LITERATURE QUIZ

LITERATURE QUIZ

SUJATA RAY

RUPA

Published by
Rupa Publications India Pvt. Ltd 2004
7/16, Ansari Road, Daryaganj
New Delhi 110002

Sales Centres:

Allahabad Bengaluru Chennai
Hyderabad Jaipur Kathmandu
Kolkata Mumbai

ISBN: 978-81-716-7016-1

Thirteenth impression 2016

20 19 18 17 16 15 14 13

The moral right of the authors has been asserted.

Printed at B. B. Press, Noida

This book is dedicated to the buyer

PREFACE

A quiz book not only tests one's knowledge of a perticular subject, but also sends one on a voyage of discovery of interesting new authors and promising new books through its questions. In a literature quiz book such leaders can be many and I hope this one will introduce you to some authors and books you would like to explore.

I have tried to include as many facets of literature from as many countries as possible, within the scope of 1000 questions.

Delhi
January 1990   SR

CONTENTS

1

FAMOUS AND INFAMOUS STATEMENTS

1. Who thinks 'Early to rise and early to bed makes a
   male healthy, wealthy and dead'?
   (a) James Thurber (b) Spike Milligan (c) Peter Sellers
   (d) Ogden Nash

2. 'To the man-in-the street, who, I am sorry to say,
   Is a keen observer of life,
   The word "intellectual" suggests straight away
   A man who's untrue to his wife.'
   Who made this observation?
   (a) W.H. Auden (b) Kingsley Amis (c) Ted Hughes
   (d) Philip Larkin

3. 'We all have sufficient strength to bear other
   people's misfortunes', wrote a hard-headed realist.
   Who is he?
   (a) Montaigne (b) Francis Bacon (c) La
   Rochefoucauld (d) Jonathan Swift

4. 'Read over your compositions, and where ever you
   meet with a passage which you think is particularly

11

fine, strike it out.' Who gave this excellent advice?
(a) Alexander Pope (b) Dr. Johnson (c) Jonathan Swift (d) F.R. Leavis

5. 'No man but a blockhead ever wrote, except for money.' Who made this remark?
(a) Barbara Cartland (b) Alexander Pope (c) Agatha Christie (d) Dr. Johnson

6. When a gentleman who was very unhappy in marriage married a second time soon after his first wife's death, someone commented that 'it was the triumph of hope over experience.' Who?
(a) John Donne (b)Shelley (c) Dr. Johnson (d) W.H. Auden

7. Whose dying words were, 'Crito, I owe a cock to Asclepius; will you remember to pay the debt'?
(a) Aristotle (b) Plato (c) Socrates (d) Aristotle Socrates Onassis

8. 'T.S. Eliot is quite at a loss
When clubwomen bustle across
At literary teas
Crying:- "What, if you please,
Did you mean by the *Mill on the Floss* ?"'
Who wrote this?
(a) W.H. Auden (b) Philip Larkin (c) Ogden Nash (d) John Betjeman

9. Who said, 'Whom God wishes to destroy, he first

makes mad'?
(a) Euripides (b) Seneca (c) Socrates (d) Dr. Johnson

10. Whose translation of Hippocrates's saying *'Ars longa, vita brevis'* is this?
'Art is long, and time is fleeting'.
(a) Pope (b) Dr. Johnson (c) Dryden (d) Longfellow

11. 'My aunt died of influenza: So they said ….But it's my belief they done the old woman in.' — Who says this?
(a) Sam Weller in *Pickwick Papers* (b) Eliza in *Pygmalion* (c) Miriam in *Sons and Lovers* (d) Molly Seagrim in *Tom Jones*

12. 'Unintelligible, the borrowings cheap and the notes useless', wrote F.L. Lucas in *New Statesman and Nation* about an important book. Which is it?
(a) Ezra Pound's *Cantos* (b) T.S. Eliot's *The Waste Land* (c) Sir James Frazer's *Golden Bough* (d) Arthur Waley's *A Hundred and Seventy Chinese Poems*

13. 'The work of a queasy undergraduate scratching his pimples' — Who made this remark about James Joyce's *Ulysses*?
(a) Virginia Woolf (b) D.H. Lawrence (c) F.R. Leavis (d) Wyndham Lewis

14. Whose advice was, 'Gather ye rosebuds while ye may'?
(a) Robert Herrick (b) Ben Jonson (c) James Shirley

(d) Sir Walter Raleigh

15. 'Fools rush in where angels fear to tread',
    'To err is human, to forgive divine', and
    'Hope springs eternal in the human breast'—
    These three statements have attained proverbial
    status. Who wrote them originally?
    (a) Francis Bacon (b) La Rochefoucauld (c) Alexan-
    der Pope (d) Dr. Johnson

16. Who could have uttered the witticism,
    'Nothing spoils a romance so much as a sense of
    humour in the woman.'
    (a) J.M. Whistler (b) John Wilkes (c) Oscar Wilde
    (d) George Bernard Shaw

17. This is a well-known quotation, and perhaps what it
    says is true : 'Marriage is popular because it
    combines the maximum of temptation with the
    maximum of opportunity.' Who said it?
    (a) Oscar Wilde (b) George Bernard Shaw (c) Aubrey
    Beardsley (d) Evelyn Waugh

18. 'Curioser and curioser' is a phrase now much used
    in smart journalism. Where does it come from?
    (a) *The Adventures of Tom Sawyer* (b) Joyce's *Ulysses*
    (c) *Alice in Wonderland* (d) *How To Be an Alien*

19. 'I do not love thee, Doctor Fell,
    The reason why I cannot tell;
    But this alone I know full well,

I do not love thee, Doctor Fell.'
This little doggerel has become famous, although few people would recall the name of the author. Can you?
(a) Benjamin Jowett (b) Lewis Carroll (c) Thomas Brown (d) Dr. Johnson

20. Who wrote, 'Some books are to be tasted, others to be swallowed, and some few to be chewed and digested'?
(a) Joseph Addison (b) Francis Bacon (c) Dr. Johnson (d) Charles Lamb

21. That was when books were being banned as obscene, left, right, and centre, and one person, fed up with it all, defined obscenity as 'whatever gives a judge an erection'. But who said, 'Obscenity can be found in every book except the telephone directory'?
(a) George Bernard Shaw (b) George Orwell (c) D.H. Lawrence (d) Henry Miller

22. 'She is as headstrong as an allegory on the banks of Nile.' Who could have said this?
(a) Dr. Spooner (b) Mrs. Skinner (c) Miss Mitford (d) Mrs. Malaprop

23. Who said, 'Patriotism is the last refuge of a scoundrel'?
(a) Thomas Carlyle (b) Dr. Johnson (c) Matthew Arnold (d) Winston Churchill

24. 'No! I am not Prince Hamlet, nor was meant to be;
Am an attendant lord.'
— Who says this?
(a) Polonius in *Hamlet* (b) Rosencrantz in *Hamlet*
(c) Prufrock in the 'Love Song' (d) A.C. Bradley in
Shakespearean Tragedy

25. 'Get stewed
Books are a load of crap.'
Who could have said this?
(a) Adolf Hitler (b) Brendan Behan (c) Philip Larkin
(d) Richard Nixon

26. Who said, 'Beware of all enterprises that require
new clothes'?
(a) Tom Paine (b) Bernard Shaw (c) Robert Frost
(d) H.D. Thoreau

27. A poet wrote an epigram 'On His Books':
'When I am dead, I hope it may be said:
His sins were scarlet, but his books were read.'
There is a reference to scarlet as the colour of sin.
Where does it come from?
(a) Stendhal : *Scarlet and Black* (b) Hawthorne : *The
Scarlet Letter* (c) Butler : *The Way of All Flesh* (d) Isaiah

28. Which is the correct rendering of Gertrude Stein's
(a) Rose is a rose is a rose (b) A rose is a rose is a rose
(c) Rose is a rose is a rose is a rose (d) A rose is a rose
is a rose is a rose?

29. Who is the author of the remark, 'the difference between journalism and literature is that journalism is unreadable and literature is not read'?
(a) Mark Twain (b) George Bernard Shaw (c) Kingsley Martin (d) Oscar Wilde

30. Who gave these definitions :
'Geography is about maps,
But biography is about chaps'?
(a) E.C. Bentley (b) Ogden Nash (c) Hilaire Belloc (d) E.E. Cummings

31. 'The dullard's envy of brilliant men is always assuaged by the suspicion that they will come to a bad end'. Who wrote this?
(a) Dr. Johnson (b) Jane Austen (c) George Bernard Shaw (d) Max Beerbohm

32. 'An egg boiled very soft is not unwholesome' — Who made this very wise observation?
(a) Jane Austen (b) Dr. Johnson (c) P.G. Wodehouse (d) Charles Dickens

33. Who said, 'The tigers of wrath are wiser than the horses of instruction'?
(a) William Blake (b) Samuel Smiles (c) Thoma. Carlyle (d) Jane Austen

34. 'Men are so honest, so thoroughly square;
Eternally noble, historically fair.'
Right or wrong, who says so?

(a) Jack Higgins (b) Henry Higgins (c) Harriet Smith
(d) Frank Harris

35. Who described *Mona Lisa* as 'older than the rocks
among which she sits'?
(a) S.T. Coleridge (b) William Morris (c) Walter Pater
(d) John Ruskin

36. Who said, 'A cynic is a man who knows the price of
everything and the value of nothing'?
(a) Oscar Wilde (b) George Bernard Shaw (c) Winston Churchill (d) Bertrand Russell

37. 'Abandon all hope, you who enter here.'
What is the source?
(a) Milton's *Paradise Lost* (b) Dante's *Divine Comedy*
(c) The main gate of Auschwitz concentration camp
(d) The gate of Sing Sing prison

38. 'You will find that the woman who is really kind to
dogs is always one who has failed to inspire
sympathy in men.' Who made this astute
observation?
(a) George Bernard Shaw (b) Gertrude Stein (c) Max
Beerbohm (d) Kingsley Amis

39. 'No great artist ever sees things as they are. If he did
he would cease to be an artist.' This particular
author made several pronouncements on art and the
artist's place in society. Who is he?
(a) George Bernard Shaw (b) Oscar Wilde (c) Jean-

Paul Sartre (d) Wyndham Lewis

40. At a political meeting a heckler told the candidate, 'I'd sooner vote for the devil than you'. The candidate replied, 'And what if your friend isn't running'? Who could the wit be?
(a) John Wilkes (b) Benjamin Disraeli (c) Winston Churchill (d) George Bernard Shaw

41. 'No man lives in vain. The history of the world is but the biography of great men.' — Whose view of history is this.
(a) John Stuart Mill (b) Samuel Johnson (c) Thomas Carlyle (d) Lytton Strachey

42. 'If a writer has to rob his mother, he will not hesitate; the "Ode on a Grecian Urn" is worth any number of old ladies.'
Whose view is this?
(a) Ernest Hemingway (b) William Faulkner (c) Saul Bellow (d) John Updike

43. Whose dying words were, 'Give Dayrolles [a visitor] a chair'?
(a) Lord Byron (b) Emily Dickinson (c) Lord Chesterfield (d) Robert Louis Stevenson

44. 'Nuptial love maketh mankind; friendly love perfecteth it; but wanton love corrupteth and embaseth it.' Who said so?
(a) Socrates (b) Shakespeare (c) Bacon (d) The Old

Testament

45. 'But at my back I always hear
Time's winged chariot hurrying near...'
— whose lines are these?
(a) Andrew Marvell (b) T.S. Eliot (c) Richard
Lovelace (d) Christopher Fry

46. 'Everyman, I will go with thee and be thy guide,
In thy most need to go by thy side.'
Who said this?
(a) Plato (b) Mr. J.M. Dent (c) Anonymous
(d) Aristotle

47. 'Any man's death diminishes me, because I am
involved in Mankind; And therefore never send to
know for whom the bell tolls, it tolls for thee.'
Who is the author of this epigraph to Hemingway's
famous novel *For Whom the Bell Tolls*?
(a) Ecclesiastes (b) John Donne (c) Gerard Manley
Hopkins (d) Dr. Johnson

48. Who said, 'The true artist will let his wife starve, his
children go barefoot, his mother drudge for his
living at seventy, sooner than work at anything but
his art'?
(a) John Keats (b) Oscar Wilde (c) George Bernard
Shaw (d) George Orwell

49. Who could have said, 'Sex is one of the nine reasons
for reincarnation....The other eight are

unimportant ?
(a) Frank Harris (b) Arthur Miller (c) Henry Miller
(d) Kingsley Amis

50. Whose dying words were, 'I am dying as I have lived, beyond my means'?
(a) Mark Twain (b) Stephen Leacock (c) Oscar Wilde
(d) P.G. Wodehouse

51. Who made the famous quip, 'Men seldom make passes at girls who wear glasses'?
(a) George Bernard Shaw (b) Dorothy Parker
(c) Lady Ottoline Morrell (d) Oscar Wilde

52. Who said 'An unexamined life is not worth living'?
(a) Socrates (b) Plato (c) Aristotle (d) Zeno

53. 'It beareth the name of Vanity Fair, because the town where 'tis kept is lighter than vanity.' The author of this quotation?
(a) John Bunyan (b) W.M. Thackeray (c) II Corinthians (d) Samuel Butler

54. "My country right or wrong" is a thing no patriot would think of saying except in a desperate case. It is like saying, "My mother drunk or sober".' Who said this?
(a) George Bernard Shaw (b) Bertrand Russell
(c) Winston Churchill (d) G.K. Chesterton

55. 'What is truth? said jesting Pilate; and would not

stay for an answer.' Where does this occur?
(a) St. John (b) Aldous Huxley (c) St. Mark
(d) Francis Bacon

56. This comes from a rationalist who exploded many modern myths: 'The fact that an opinion has been widely held is no evidence whatsoever that it is not utterly absurd'. Who wrote it?
(a) George Bernard Shaw (b) Bertrand Russell
(c) Albert Einstein (d) A.J.P. Taylor

57. 'It's most dangerous nowadays for a husband to pay any attention to his wife in public. It always makes people think that he beats her when they are alone.' Who said this about behaviour in polite society?
(a) Oscar Wilde (b) George Bernard Shaw (c) Mark Twain (d) James Thurber

58. Not everybody is a believer in the holiness of love. Who said, 'Love is only the dirty trick played on us to achieve continuation of the species'?
(a) George Bernard Shaw (b) W.H. Auden (c) E.M. Forster (d) W. Somerset Maugham

59. 'Be nice to people on your way up because you'll meet 'em on your way down.' Whose sensible advice is this?
(a) Wilson Mizner (b) Ring Lardner (c) Mark Twain
(d) Dorothy Parker

60. 'For now we see through a glass, darkly, but then

face to face; now I know in part; but then shall I know even as also I am known.' Many phrases and book titles have been coined by varying the expression 'through a glass, darkly.' Where does the full quotation occur?
(a) Bacon's *Essays* (b) Paul to Corinthians, First Epistle (c) Sir Thomas More's *Utopia* (d) Hooker: *Ecclesiastical Polity*

61. In a short poem of two stanzas, the second states scathingly:
'How dreary to be somebody!
How public, like a frog
To tell your name the livelong day
To an admiring bog!'
Who is the poet?
(a) Amy Lowell (b) Emily Dickinson (c) H.D. (d) Marianne Moore

62. ' "But I should like to come", Miss Spence protested, throwing a rapid Gioconda at him.' This quote really gives it away by using one word; nevertheless, who is the author?
(a) Agatha Christie (b) Graham Greene (c) Christopher Isherwood (d) Aldous Huxley

63. Doublethink, which means the power of holding two contrary beliefs in one's mind simultaneously, and accepting both of them was so defined by
(a) C. Northcote Parkinson (b) Bertrand Russell

(c) George Orwell (d) George Bernard Shaw

64. 'A single sentence will suffice for modern man: he fornicated and read the papers.'
Where does this cynical summing up occur?
(a) Colin Wilson : *The Outsider* (b) Albert Camus : *The Fall* (c) Jean-Paul Sartre : *The Age of Reason* (d) H.G. Wells : *The History of Mr. Polly*

65. 'His appeal is to readers with a lifelong appetite for juvenile trash.' Who is Edmund Wilson talking about?
(a) A.A. Milne (b) Robert Louis Stevenson (c) J.R.R. Tolkien (d) C.S. Lewis

66. ' "I don't", she added, "know anything about music, really. But I know what I like".' Millions of Philistines have said the same thing about music, poetry, abstract art, and a host of other creative arts since 1911 when this was written. Who is the author?
(a) George Bernard Shaw (b) Oscar Wilde (c) Virginia Woolf (d) Max Beerbohm

67. 'A cold coming they had of it.' Where does this originally occur?
(a) T.S. Eliot's 'The Journey of the Magi' (b) St. Augustine's *Confessions* (c) Lancelot Andrewes' 'Sermon on the Nativity' (d) Miracle plays of the Chester cycle

68. 'Cut out all those exclamation marks. An

exclamation mark is like laughing at your own joke.'
Who is the author, and practitioner of this sound bit
of advice on punctuation?
(a) Kingsley Amis (b) J.P. Donleavy (c) F. Scott
Fitzgerald (d) Ernest Hemingway

69. 'They fuck you up, your mum and dad.
They may not mean to, but they do.
They fill you with the faults they had
And add some extra, just for you.'
From the uninhibited use of language you can guess
that this must have been written after 1960. Who is
the poet?
(a) Ted Hughes (b) Philip Larkin (c) Thom Gunn
(d) R.S. Thomas

70. 'A touch of cold in the Autumn night—
I walked abroad,
And saw the ruddy moon lean over a hedge
Like a red-faced farmer.
I did not stop to speak, but nodded,
And round about were the wistful stars
With white faces like town children.'
This is perhaps the most famous imagist poem. Who
wrote it?
(a) H.D. (b) Richard Aldingto (c) T.E. Hulme
(d) Ezra Pound

71. 'If my mother had lived, I could not have loved you,
for she would never have let me go.' D.H. Lawrence
told his wife Frieda. In which novel does Lawrence

portray a mother's possessive love for her son?
(a) *The Trespasser* (b) *The Rainbow* (c) *Sons and Lovers*
(d) *The Lost Girl*

2. Hardy added a subtitle to his novel *Tess of the D'Urbervilles* as his personal statement. What is it?
(a) *A Maid's Tragedy* (b) *A Pure Woman* (c) *A Plaything of Fate* (d) *A Tragedy of the Innocent*

2

CURIOSER AND CURIOSER

73. A famous German author received the following letter from his publisher: 'Dear Herr Doktor, You are already 18 months behind time with the manuscript of ...which you have agreed to write for us. If we do not receive the manuscript within six months, we shall be obliged to commission another author to do the work.' Which manuscript could it be?

    (a) *Buddenbrooks* by Thomas Mann (b) *Faust* by Goethe (c) Freud's *Interpretation of Dreams* (d) Karl Marx : *Das Kapital*

74. 'I have seen, and heard much of cockney impudence before now; but never expected to hear a coxcomb ask two hundred guineas for flinging a pot of paint in the public's face' — wrote an art critic about a painting. The painter sued him. In the court the defence counsel asked. 'For two days' labour you ask two hundred guineas?' The painter replied, 'No, I ask it for the knowledge of a lifetime.' He won the case. Who is the painter?

(a) J.M.W. Turner (b) John Constable (c) J.m. Whistler (d) J.E. Millais

75. The name of Kit-Kat club was derived from Christopher Cat's mutton pies, and it was at his shop that its members, poets, dramatists, and essayists assembled. Who were the members?
(a) Pope, Steele, Addison, Congreve... (b) Johnson, Boswell, Goldsmith, Reynolds... (c) Auden, MacNeice, Spender... (d) Oscar Wilde, Whistler, Aubrey Beardsley...

76. *Memoirs of a Woman of Pleasure,* or *Fanny Hill*, the name by which it is popularly known, brought its publisher £ 10,000 (in 1748-49). How much could the author, John Cleland, have earned?
(a) £ 21 (b) £ 128 (c) £ 860 (d) £ 2200

77. The mother of one of the following had the same name as a famous perfume. Whose?
(a) William Shakespeare (b) Thomas Hardy (c) John Arden (d) Kingsley Amis

78. Corruption is now a way of life for the successful and it has numerous practitioners and aspirers. In the seventeenth century, however, it made startling news. This eminent literary figure, first a barrister, then Solicitor-General, and finally judge, was accused of bribery and admitted his guilt. He was fined, dismissed and imprisoned — such was the strange code of public life in those days. Who was

he?
(a) Sir Philip Sidney (b) Edmund Spenser
(c) Francis Bacon (d) Sir Thomas Wyatt

79. Don Juan, the proverbial heartless seducer, has been celebrated by poets, dramatists, and musicians like Byron, Browning, Pushkin, Shaw, and Mozart — among others. Don Juan, however, had a much-injured wife. What is her name?
(a) Anna (b) Elvira (c) Maria (d) Esmerelda

80. Only one of the following was not conceived in dreams. Which?
(a) Coleridge's *Kubla Khan* (b) Mary Shelley's *Frankenstein* (c) Wilkie Collins's *The Moonstone* (d) R.L. Stevenson's *Dr. Jekyll and Mr. Hyde*

81. Match the Latinate Doctors with their real names:
1. Doctor Angelicus (a) Roger Bacon 2. Doctor Invincibilis (b) St. Thomas Aquinas 3. Doctor Mirabilis (c) Duns Scotus 4. Doctor Subtilis (d) William of Ockham

82. *Alice's Adventures in Wonderland* originated from a boat trip which the Christ Church lecturer in mathematics took with the three daughters of the Dean of Christ Church. Who were the three daughters?
(a) Lorina, Alice, and Edith (b) Martha, Selina, and Alice (c) Marina, Serena, and Alice (d) Joan, Mary, and Alice

83. How is the name Houyhnhnms, Swift's rational horses in *Gulliver's Travels*, pronounced?
(a) Who—hoon-hoon-moos (b) Why—nims (c) Whinnims (d) Whooms

84. What was Arthur Conan Doyle's profession in real life?
(a) Engineer (b) Doctor (c) Professional Detective (d) Stockbroker

85. Where were Arthur Conan Doyle's stories mostly published?
(a) *The Gentleman's Magazine* (b) *The Cornhill Magazine* (c) *Bentley's Miscellany* (d) *The Strand Magazine*

86. Which city in the U.S. has banned the largest number of books on moral grounds?
(a) New York (b) Chicago (c) Boston (d) Jackson, Mississippi

87. *Incunabula* means
(a) A child's writing (b) Books produced in the infancy of printing from moveable types (c) Children's literature (d) Books about child rearing, e.g., Dr. Spock's books.

88. Three of the following writers were banished from their countries for what they wrote. Who is the exception?
(a) Euripides (b) Plato (c) Aristotle (d) Ovid

89. 'Burned by the common hangman' is a phrase used of proscribed books. Which was the first such recorded burning in England?
(a) 1497; the works of Ovid, Propertius, Boccaccio and others (b) 1554; *The Historie of Italie* (c) 1579; John Stubbs' attack on the proposed marriage of Queen Elizabeth (d) 1660; John Milton's *Pro Populo Anglicano Defensio*, and *Eikonoklastes*

90. In 1929 the Soviet Union banned an English writer for 'occultism and spiritualism'. Who is the writer?
(a) William Shakespeare (b) Charles Dickens (c) Sir Arthur Conan Doyle (d) Thomas Hardy

91. There is a legend about a lexicographer caught kissing a chambermaid by his wife. 'Why..., I am *surprised* !' his wife is supposed to have said. 'Madame,' he corrected her, '*You* are astonished, *I* am surprised,' Who is he?
(a) Dr. Johnson (b) Noah Webster (c) Sir James Murray (d) H.W. Fowler

92. Which common distinction did these authors share: Giosue Corducci, R.C. Eucken, W.S. Reymont, and Nelly Sachs?
(a) They were all one-book authors (b) The were all mystery story writers (c) They were all Nobel Prize winners (d) They were all Pulitzer Prize winners

93. Bowdlerize means
(a) Bowling the reader over with startling writing

(b) Using large portions of a book in another without acknowledgement (c) A publisher changing the ending of a novel because it thinks it knows better than the author (d) Removing all references considered to be indecent or blasphemous from a book

94. What is a blurb?
(a) Information about a book in a publisher's advertisement (b) A short review (c) Description of a book's contents printed on the flap of the jacket or any part of the book (d) A damaging review

95. Which reference book reigns as the all-time bestseller?
(a) *The Concise Oxford Dictionary* (b) *Bartholomew's World Atlas* (c) *The Guinness Book of Records* (d) *Webster's Collegiate Dictionary*

96. Who acted the part of Eliza Doolittle in the film version of Shaw's *Pygmalion, My Fair Lady*?
(a) Sophia Loren (b) Grace Kelly (c) Elizabeth Taylor (d) Audrey Hepburn

97. Which of the following languages are dead, i.e., not spoken in everyday use by a large enough number of people?
(a) Cornish (b) Afrikaans (c) Latin (d) Yiddish

98. How many christian names did Oscar Wilde have?
(a) 1 (b) 2 (c) 3 (d) 4

99. Of the following, who is the most translated author of the world?
(a) Leo Tolstoy (b) Agatha Christie (c) Mao Tse Tung (d) V.I. Lenin

100. How many books did Agatha Christie write?
(a) 87 (b) 90 (c) 215 (d) 78

101. What was the price of Penguins when they were first published?
(a) 6d. (b) 9d. (c) 1/6 (d) 2/6

102. In which film of Eugene O'Neill did Paul Robeson, the singer, play a star part?
(a) *The Hairy Ape* (b) *The Great God Brown* (c) *The Iceman Cometh* (d) *Emperor Jones*

103. Which is the most frequently used English word in writing?
(a) and (b) to (c) the (d) a

104. Which is the letter of the English alphabet which occurs least often in writing?
(a) j (b) w (c) x (d) z

105. Which is the letter of the English alphabet which occurs most often in writing?
(a) s (b) r (c) a (d) e

106. Of all these countries which banned Mickey Mouse, one did so on the grounds that it was 'an

anti-red rebel'. Which?
(a) Nazi Germany (b) Soviet Union (c) Yugoslavia
(d) East Germany

107. What did Lord Byron, A.C.Swinburne, Edgar Allan
Poe, and Eugene O'Neill have in common?
(a) All died at the age of 36 (b) They were all nobly
born (c) They were all married more than once
(d) All were powerful swimmers.

108. Stalin, who professed to be a patron of arts,
intervened to save many artists, of one of whom he
said, 'Do not touch this cloud-dweller'. Who is he?
(a) Mikhail Bulgakov (b) Dmitri Shostakovich
(c) Alexander Solzhenitsyn (d) Boris Pasternak

109. What have the following persons in common: R.C.
Eucken, Paul Heyse, C.F.G. Spitteler, and W.S.
Reymont?
(a) Writers of off-Broadway plays (b) Characters in
Henry James's novels (c) Characters in Dickens's
American Notes (d) Recipients of the Nobel Prize in
Literature

110. Where authors prefer to use initials in signing their
names, it is wrong to refer to them by their full
names. Which of the following are wrong?
(a) David Herbert Lawrence (b) Edward Morgan
Foster (c) Edward Estlin Cummings (d) Thomas
Stearns Eliot

111. Whose dying words were, 'I've had 18 straight whiskies. . . . I think that's the record'?
(a) F. Scott Fitzgerald (b) Ernest Hemingway (c) Eugene O'Neill (d) Dylan Thomas

112. Who used to say to her dog, 'Play Hemingway. Be fierce'?
(a) Dorothy Parker (b) Gertrude Stein (c) Emily Post (d) Nancy Mitford

113. Autobiographies of people who think their lives may have some lessons for others abound in literature. Who wrote: 'Only when one has lost all curiosity about the future has one reached the age to write an autobiography'?
(a) Somerset Maugham (b) Aldous Huxley (c) Evelyn Waugh (d) Kingsley Amis

114. Charles Dickens was the first editor of a newspaper which started in 1846. Which was it?
(a)*The Morning Chronicle* (b)*Daily News* (c)*Morning Post* (d)*Daily Chronicle*

115. *The Autobiography of Alice B. Toklas*, who was a secretary, was actually the autobiography of her employer. Who is the employer?
(a) Marianne Moore (b) Emily Post (c) Hilda Doolittle (d) Gertrude Stein

116. Ariel, the airy spirit in Shakspeare's *Tempest*, lends his name to a famous biography by Andre'

Maurois. Whose?
(a) Coleridge's (b) Byron's (c) Shelley's (d) Keats's

117. James Morris's trilogy on the Raj has three of the following books. Which is the intruder?
(a) *Heaven's Command* (b) *Rule Britannia* (c) *Pax Britannica* (d) *Farewell the Trumpets*

118. Who is the author of this famous saying, 'Mad dogs and Englishmen go out in the midday sun'?
(a) Noel Coward (b) Peter Sellers (c) James Agee (d) Emily Dickinson

119. Who was called 'English Literature's performing flea'?
(a) George Bernard Shaw (b) Noel Coward (c) P.G. Wodehouse (d) Muriel Spark

120. Who was the 'Swan of Lichfield'?
(a) Dr. Johnson (b) William Shakespeare (c) Anna Sewell (d) Anna Seward

121. Keats speaks of 'Stout Cortez, when with eagle eyes/ He stared at the Pacific'. He was staring from Darien in Panama. Eyeing which country to ransack?
(a) Costa Rica (b) Peru (c) Guatemala (d) Mexico

122. Match the words with their meanings:
1. Bibliopole   (a) One who hoards books
2. Bibliotaph (b) Destroyer of books 3. Biblioclast

(c) Bookseller 4. Bibliomaniac (d) A book collector who loves books to the point of madness

123. 'Dictionaries are like watches. The worst is better than none, and the best cannot be expected to go quite true.' Which lexicographer said this?
(a) Dr. Johnson (b) Noah Webster (c) Sir James Murray (d) H.W. Fowler

124. What does redux in the Updike novel *Rabbit Redux* mean?
(a) Renewed health after sickness (b) Ill (c) Impoverished (d) Ridiculous

125. Arcadia—the traditional location of the idealized world of the pastoral—was first described by
(a) Vergil (b) Sir Philip Sidney (c) Theocritus (d) Edmund Spenser

126. Among the earliest feminist literature was *A Vindication of the Rights of Woman* (1792), whose author was called by someone 'a hyena in petticoats'. Who is she?
(a) George Eliot (b) Mary Godwin (c) Mary Wollstonecraft (d) Mrs Thrale

127. All, except one of the following, were first published anonymously. Which is the exception?
(a) Fielding: *Joseph Andrews* (b) Byron: *Don Juan* (c) Tennyson: *In Memoriam* (d) John Cleland: *Fanny Hill*

128. The Devil's Dictionary defines a bore as 'a person who talks when you wish him to listen', and patience as 'a minor form of despair, disguised as a virtue'. Peace, in international affairs is 'a period of

cheating between two periods of fighting'. Who wrote this dictionary?
(a) Ambrose Bierce (b) Washington Irving (c) Jonathan Swift (d) Oscar Wilde

129. 'All art constantly aspires towards the condition of music.' Who made this observation?
(a) Clive Bell (b) Herbert Read (c) Walter Pater (d) Benjamin Britten

130. Match the meanings of these preposterous words:
1. onochalasia (a) fear of hearing a certain word
2. onomasticon (b) buying as a means of mental relaxation 3. onomatophobia (c) a dictionary
4. onolatry (d) ass-worship

131. Match the meanings of these vaguely familiar words.
1. hogshead (a) an effeminate-looking man
2. philalethist (b) buttocks 3. nates (c) a truth-lover 4. twiddlepoop (d) a measure of 63 gallons

132. Like and dislike seem to be indiscriminately (not to one who knows Latin) attached to the first syllable of the following words. Find their right meanings.
1. philauty (a) a woman who dislikes kissing
2. philematophobe (b) pertaining to care of hair
3. philocomal (c) lover of prostitutes 4.philopornist (d) self-love

133. *Pilgrim's Progress* by John Bunyan, published in

1678, priced at 1s.6d, sold very well. In the first ten years it sold
(a) more than 5000 copies (b) more than 12000 copies (c) more than 100,000 copies (d) extremely well, but somewhat less than 50,000 copies

134. When did the first complete book printed from moveable type appear in Europe?
(a) 1384 (b) 1456 (c) 1475 (d) 1477

135. Who was the first recipient of the Nobel Prize for Literature?
(a) Theodor Mommsen (b) Leo Tolstoy (c) R.F.A. Sully-Prudhomme (d) Rudyard Kipling

136. Who was the only Laureate to refuse the Nobel Prize?
(a) Boris Pasternak (b) Pablo Neruda (c) Albert Camus (d) Jean-Paul Sartre

137. Which is the country which stocks the largest number of library books?
(a) U.S.S.R. (b) U.S.A. (c) France (d) U.K.

138. Which is now the world's largest library?
(a) The Bodleian Library, Oxford (b) The British Museum Library, London (c) Bibliotheque Nationale, Paris (d) The Library of Congress, Washington

139. Among literature (in its broad sense) distributed

free which has the largest circulation?
(a) Quotations from the Works of Mao Tse-Tung
(b) Sears, Roebuck Catalog (c) The Truth That Leads
to Eternal Life (Jehovah's Witnesses) (d) The Bible

140. Which is the maximum number of *consecutive*
vowels to be found in an English word? Give the
number and the word.
(a) 3 (b) 4 (c) 5 (d) 6

141. When did the last case of book burning occur?
(a) 1933 (b) 1939 (c) 1946 (d) 1965

142. The Oxford English Dictionary (OED) was
conceived in 1858. When was it completed?
(a) 1904 (b) 1919 (c) 1928 (d) 1936

143. The crime and mystery writer Nicholas Blake was
really a well-known poet. Choose the right name.
(a) Cecil Day Lewis (b) W.H. Auden (c) Louis
MacNeice (d) Thom Gunn

144. The Kelmscott Press, which was started in 1890,
soon became famous for its distinctive type
designs, page borders and fine binding. Who was
the founder?
(a) John Ruskin (b) William Morris (c) Aubrey
Beardsley (d) Sir Stanley Unwin

145. Only one of the following won the Nobel Prize for
Literature. Who?

(a) Joseph Conrad (b) Rainer Maria Rilke (c) Knut Hamsun (d) Marcel Proust

146. One of Agatha Christie's stories had the longest run of any play, with over 10,000 performances. Which?
(a) *Murder on the Orient Express* (b) *Arsenic and Old Lace* (c) *The Mousetrap* (d) *The Murder at the Vicarage*

147. Who is the father of American lexicography?
(a) Noah Webster (b) Merriam Webster (c) Charles Random (d) Wilfred Funk

148. How many titles were there in the first lot of Penguins published?
(a) 10 (b) 12 (c) 6 (d) 18

149. Who started the Left Book Club?
(a) V.K. Krishna Menon (b) Leonard Woolf (c) Victor Gollancz (d) Harry Pollitt

150. Eugenio Montale (1896-1981) was the Nobel Prize winner in Literature in 1975. To which country did this poet and critic belong?
(a) Italy (b) Spain (c) Portugal (d) Mexico

151. When was the first book printed in England and by whom?
(a) 1384 (b) 1456 (c) 1475 (d) 1477

152. When did the best-known American paperback house, Pocket Books, start?
(a) Five years before Penguin (b) The same year as Penguin (c) Four years after Penguin (d) 1941

153. The fictional detective Sherlock Holmes lived at
(a) 221 Baker Street, London (b) 212 Baker Street, London (c) 122 B Baker Street, London (d) 221 B Baker Street, London

154. This lady burnt all her husband's unpublished works and journals after her husband's death, as she considered them obscene. Who is she?
(a) The Earl of Rochester's wife (b) Mary Shelley, the wife of the poet Shelley (c) James Joyce's wife (d) Sir Richard Burton's wife

155. When was the Nobel Prize for Literature first awarded?
(a) 1901 (b) 1908 (c) 1919 (d) 1898

156. Who published the first unexpurgated edition of Lawrence's *Lady Chatterley's Lover* in Britain?
(a) Victor Gollancz (b) John Calder (c) Faber and Faber (d) Penguin Books

157. Of the following books which is considered to be all-time paperback bestseller?
(a) *Great Gatsby* (b) *The Thornbirds* (c) *The Secret Diary of Adrian Mole Aged* $13\frac{3}{4}$ (d) *Pocket Book of Baby and Child Care*

158. Of the following Pocket Book titles issued among the first ten, which had the largest sale in the first eighteen years?
(a) Emily Bronte : *Wuthering Heights* (b) James Hilton : *Lost Horizon* (c) Shakespeare : *Five Great Tragedies* (d) Agatha Christie : *The Murder of Roger Ackroyd*

159. The surname of Charlotte Bronte's heroine Jane Eyre is pronounced
(a) Air (b)Ira (c) Ear (d) Ay-rie

160. When was the ban on the publication of the unexpurgated version of Lawrence's *Lady Chatterley's Lover* lifted in Britain?
(a) 1960 (b) 1964 (c) 1968 (d) 1978

161. Of the four dictionaries mentioned here which preceded the others?
(a) Webster's *Compendious Dictionary of the English Language* (b) Dr. Johnson's *Dictionary of the English Language* (c) Bailey's *Universal Etymological English Dictionary* (d) Webster's *Spelling Book*

162. Which is the first magazine to be called a magazine?
(a) *Gentleman's Magazine* (b) *Cornhill Magazine* (c) *Harper's Magazine* (d) *McClure's Magazine*

163. When did Penguin books first come out?

(a) 1930 (b) 1935 (c) 1938 (d) 1940

164. For what is the Pulitzer prize awarded?
(a) Literature (b) Plays for the theatre (c) Journalism
(d) Film scripts

165. The following are some improbable book titles. All except one have been published. Which is the exception?
(a) *Proceedings of the Second International Workshop on Nude Mice* (b) *Do It Yourself Brain Surgery and Other Home Skills* (c) *Causes, Prevention, and Cure of Nosepicking* (d) *Sex after Death*

3

BIOGRAPHY IS ABOUT CHAPS

166. Three of the following authors died of over-indulgence in food and drink. Who is the exception?
(a) Robert Greene (b) William Shakespeare (c) O. Henry (d) W.M. Thackeray

167. On being presented to Abraham Lincoln, he asked about this author, 'Is this the little woman whose book made such a great war?' Who is the lady?
(a) Charlotte Smith (b) Aphra Behn (c) Jane Porter (d) Harriet Beecher Stowe

168. Three of the following authors did not live to be 36, but one did, and he crossed 80. Who is the long-lived one?
(a) John Keats (b) Hart Crane (c) Ezra Pound (d) Katherine Mansfield

169. Of the following British authors, one was not born in India. Who?
(a) W.M. Thackeray (b) Rudyard Kipling (c) E.M.

Forster (d) George Orwell

170. Awarded the Nobel Prize in literature for 1983, this
novelist visited India recently. Identify his novel
from the following list and name him.
(a) *The Spire* (b) *The Mimic Man* (c) *Rites of Passage*
(d) *Dr. Fischer of Geneva Or the Bomb Party*

171. Whose epitaph is this?
'Good friend, for Jesus' sake forbear
To dig the dust enclosed here,
Blest be the man that spares these stones,
And curst be he that moves my bones'.
(a) Christopher Marlowe (b) William Shakespeare
(c) Thomas Middleton (d) Ben Jonson

172. This author frequently refused payment for his
poems as he wrote for 'glory'.
(a) Lord Byron (b) Lord Tennyson (c) John Keats
(d) P.B. Shelley

173. This detective story writer was a foundling; he was
brought up by a Billingsgate fish porter. He grew
rich, ran two Rolls Royces, and used to hire the
entire restaurant of the Carlton Hotel for his supper
parties. Of course he died in debt. *Four Just Men*
brought him fame. Who is he?
(a) Ronald Knox (b) Raymond Chandler (c) Edgar
Wallace (d) Sir Arthur Conan Doyle

174. In the Poet's Corner in Westminster Abbey are

buried many of the literary figures of Britain. One, however, was buried standing up, because he expressed such a wish in jest, but James I took him seriously.
(a) Edmund Spenser (b) Christopher Marlowe (c) William Shakespeare (d) Ben Jonson

175. Arrange the following authors chronologically, i.e., by their date of birth.
(a) Jane Austen (b) Charlotte Bronte (c) Mrs Aphra Behn (d) Emily Bronte

176. Which among the following English authors were opium addicts?
(a) Thomas De Quincey (b) Christopher Marlowe (c) Oscar Wilde (d) Samuel Taylor Coleridge

177. After a quarrel, this foul-tempered lady emptied a chamberpot on her husband's head, who merely said 'After the thunder, comes the rain'. Who is she?
(a) Xanthippe, wife of Socrates (b) Anne Hathaway, wife of Shakespeare (c) Mary Powell, wife of Milton (d) Zelda Sayre, wife of F. Scott Fitzgerald

178. On which poet's epitaph are the words engraved, 'Here lies one whose name was writ in water'?
(a) William Wordsworth (b) P.B. Shelley (c) Lord Byron (d) John Keats

179. Who was Mark Twain in real life?
(a) Charles Lutwidge Dodgson (b) Eric Blair

(c) Samuel Langhorne Clemens (d) R.C. Sheriff

180. Which British poet went to fight for Greece, but died before seeing any action?
(a) Lord Byron (b) Lord Tennyson (c) Arthur O'Shaughnessy (d) Wilfrid Scawen Blunt

181. Which of these poets was born American, but became a British citizen?
(a) T.S. Eliot (b) W.H. Auden (c) Stephen Spender (d) Louis MacNeice

182. What was the nationality of Hans Christian Andersen?
(a) Norwegian (b) Danish (c) Swedish (d) Finnish

183. Who really was the mystery writer Ellery Queen?
(a) Ellery Sedgwick (b) William Ellery Leonard (c) A Syndicate (d) Frederic Dannay

184. Who is it that Keats fell in love with and is supposed to have addressed his last sonnet to?
(a) Mary (b) Fanny (c) Jenny (d) Anne

185. What is the nationality of Wole Soyinka, the Nobel Prize-winning African author?
(a) Senegalese (b) Nigerian (c) Angolan (d) Ghanaian

186. Vladimir Mayakovsky (1893-1930), a major Russian poet of the Revolution, later became

disenchanted with Soviet life. How did he die?
(a) Shot in a purge (b) In Lubianka, insane (c) Of tuberculosis, in Gulag (d) Committed suicide

187. In which language did August Strindberg originally write?
(a) Norwegian (b) Danish (c) Finnish (d) Swedish

188. What is the nationality of Khalil Gibran (1833-1931)?
(a) Lebanese (b) Syrian (c) Persian (d) Arab

189. Samuel Beckett, author of *Waiting for Godot*, was for a long time the secretary of an Irish author. Who is that author?
(a) W.B. Yeats (b) J.M. Synge (c) James Joyce (d) Sean O'Casey

190. Although Russian was his mother tongue, he is one of the most distinguished writers of English and wrote a novel which scandalized a lot of people. He wrote *Pnin*, *Pale Fire*, and *Speak, Memory* among other books. Who is he?
(a) Alexander Solzhenitsyn (b) Boris Pasternak (c) Vladimir Nabokov (d) Ivan Denisovich

191. Three of the following authors lived to read their own obituaries in newspapers; one even telling a journalist, 'The reports of my death are highly exaggerated'. Who is the exception?
(a) Ernest Hemingway (b) Mark Twain (c) Bertrand

Russell (d) Dylan Thomas

192. *Brief Candles, The Human Situation, The Genius and the Goddess, Ape and Essence* are some of the books written by a British novelist of this century, who had extremely poor eyesight but recovered through exercises and wrote a book on it. Who is he?
(a) Aldous Huxley (b) James Joyce (c) Kingsley Amis (d) John Fowles

193. William Butler Yeats is perhaps the most famous poet of Ireland. His father, John Butler Yeats, also distinguished himself in one of the arts. Which is it?
(a) Epic Poetry (b) Sculpture (c) Portrait Painting (d) Architecture

194. How is the second name of Percy Bysshe Shelley pronounced?
(a) Bish (b) Bissi (c) Bishi (d) Bash

195. *In Memoriam* was written by a poet to mourn the death of a friend. Name the poet and the friend.
(a) Byron, on — (b) Tennyson, on — (c) T.S. Eliot, on — (d) Coleridge, on —

196. What is James Hadley Chase's real name?
(a) Linda Toogood (b) Pamela Diplomat (c) Rene Raymond (d) Roger Twit

197. Of the following writers who was the shortest?
(a) Alexander Pope (b) John Keats (c) P.B. Shelley

198. Three pairs of literary lovers are given. Complete the third.
    (a) Abelard and He'loise (b) Dante and Beatrice (c) Scott Fitzgerald and—— (d) Keats and Fanny

199. One of the following literary libertines claimed to have fathered 500 children. Who?
    (a) Alexandre Dumas (b) Frank Harris (c) Lord Byron (d) Robert Burns

200. One of the following was a non-swimmer and died by drowning. Who?
    (a) Lord Byron (b) P.B. Shelley (c) A.C. Swinburne (d) Edgar Allan Poe

201. Of the following, only one is not a pen name. Which?
    (a) Maxim Gorky (b) Mark Twain (c) George Orwell (d) Stephen Crane

202. Who was the youngest among the following poets to die?
    (a) Thomas Chatterton (b) Rupert Brooke (c) John Keats (d) Christopher Marlowe

203. How old was George Bernard Shaw when he died?
    (a) 99 (b) 96 (c) 94 (d) 91

204. Who among the following is not a Nobel Prize

winner?

(a) George Bernard Shaw (b) Samuel Beckett (c) Graham Greene (d) Odysseus Elytis

205. Which of these poets was born British, but became an American citizen?
(a) T.S. Eliot (b) W.H. Auden (c) Louis MacNeice (d) Cecil Day Lewis

206. Who was Eric Blair?
(a) Anthony Burgess (b) Aldous Huxley (c) George Orwell (d) Arthur Koestler

207. Cervantes died on 23 April 1916. On that day another famous person died. Who?
(a) Shakespeare (b) Ben Jonson (c) Christopher Marlowe (d) Francis Bacon

208. Lewis Carroll's Alice, Alice Liddell, became famous. What did her father become famous for?
(a) Writing an authoritative Greek dictionary (b) Becoming Vice-Chancellor of Oxford for six consecutive terms (c) Writing a textbook of Greek grammar (d) Founding Chirst Church College, Oxford

209. This Japanese novelist committed ritual suicide publicly after addressing the Japanese army, accusing it of powerlessness. Identify him.
(a) Junichiro Tanizaki (b) Yukiyo Mishima (c) Yasunari Kawabata (d) Kobo Abe

210. What was the profession for which Anton Chekhov was trained?
(a) Doctor (b) Engineer (c) School teacher (d) Carpenter

211. Karel Capek, the author of *R.U.R.* and *Insect Play* was a
(a) German writer (b) Austrian writer (c) Czech writer (d) Romanian writer

212. In which language did Isaae Bashevis Singer originally write?
(a) Yiddish (b) German (c) Polish (d) Hebrew

213. Who is the detective story writer Michael Innes in real life?
(a) Sir Maurice Bowra (b) F.R. Leavis (c) Helen Gardner (d) J.I.M. Stewart

214. Aldous Huxley (1894-1963) travelled a lot in his later years and visited India. In which book did he write about his visit?
(a) *Jesting Pilate* (b) *Eyeless in Gaza* (c) *The Doors of Perception* (d) *Mortal Coils*

215. The first ever utterance of this child, who later became associated with India, on being consoled by a lady who had accidently dropped hot liquid on his knee, was 'Thank you madam. The agony is much abated'. Who is he?
(a) Edmund Burke (b) T.B. Macaulay (c) Lord

Curzon (d) Rudyard Kipling

216. Which English author is supposed to have had an IQ of 190 (140 qualifies one as a genius) ?
(a) John Milton (b) John Stuart Mill (c) Gerard Manley Hopkins (d) Kingsley Amis

217. Tell who among the following was not a custom house official.
(a) Geoffrey Chaucer (b) Andrew Marvell (c) Nathaniel Hawthorne (d) Herman Melville

218. According to tradition, the real Don Juan, viz., Don Juan Tenorio, had
(a) 16,527 (b) 2594 (c) 97 (d) 2000 mistresses.

219. Only one of the following authors ever married. Who is it?
(a) Jane Austen (b) Alexander Pope (c) Henry James (d) Virginia Woolf

220. Of the following authors name those who suffered from insanity.
(a) Guy de Maupassant (b) Virginia Woolf (c) Edgar Allan Poe (d) Jonathan Swift

221. Which poet buried with his wife the little book in which he wrote all his poems, but after seven years regretted the act, had the grave opened, and recovered the poems?
These poems had excellent reviews.

(a) Robert Browning (b) Dante Gabriel Rossetti
(c) A.C. Swinburne (d) William Morris

222. Match the adopted names with the names given at
birth.
1. Joseph Conrad (a) Emily Bronte 2. Andre'
Maurois (b) Upton Sinclair 3. Ellis Bell (c) Teodor
J.K. Korzeniowsky 4. Arthur Sterling (d) Emile
Herzog

223. What do the following authors have in common:
Francois Villon, John Suckling, Thomas Otway,
John Reed?
(a) They all died at the age of 33 (b) They all suffered
imprisonment (c) They were all impoverished
poets (d) All committed suicide

224. Where was the French novelist Albert Camus born?
(a) Oran (b) Paris (c) Algiers (d) Casablanca

225. Of which country was Luis de Camoens (author of
Lusiads) the national poet?
(a) Portugal (b) Spain (c) Mexico (d) Argentina

226. Heinrich Boll, Nobel Prize winner of 1972, is the
author of *Billiards at Half Past Nine.* In which
language does he write?
(a) German (b) Polish (c) Hungarian (d) English

227. Lytton Strachey's *Eminent Victorians* is considered
to be a landmark in the history of biography. It had

four essays. Of the following five which one is bogus?
(a) Cardinal Newman (b) Cardinal Manning (c) Florence Nightingale (d) Thomas Arnold

228. Name the nationality of the 1967 Nobel Prize winner Miguel Angel Asturias.
(a) Mexican (b) Chilean (c) Guatemalan (d) Peruvian

229. Isaac Babel (1894-1941) was a Jewish storyteller who won fame with his depiction of ghetto life. What was his nationality?
(a) German (b) Russian (c) Polish (d) Israeli

230. Djuna Barnes (1892-1982), best known for *Nightwood*, a novel marked by a sense of horror and decay, also wrote the novel *Ryder*. Which country did she belong to?
(a) Colombia (b) Mexico (c) The United States (d) Chile

231. The black American author James Baldwin is famous as the author of *Go Tell It on the Mountain* and *The Fire Next Time*. When was he born?
(a) Between 1910 and 1920 (b) Between 1920 and 1930 (c) Between 1930 and 1940 (d) Between 1940 and 1950

232. S.Y. Agnon (1888-1970) was a famous Israeli writer who was awarded the Nobel Prize in 1966. In which

language did he write?
(a) Polish (b) Yiddish (c) German (d) Hebrew

233. Just before she died she asked, 'What is the answer?' When no answer came, she laughed and said, 'In that case, what is the question?' Then she died. — Who?
(a) Virginia Woolf (b) Gertrude Stein (c) Dorothy Richardson (d) Elizabeth Bowen

234. Who among the following is not a Nobel Prize winner?
(a) Thomas Hardy (b) Winston Churchill (c) Nelly Sachs (d) Harry Martinson

235. Whose dying words, when asked if a priest should be called, were, 'No, God will pardon me, that's his line of work'?
(a) John Stuart Mill (b) Heinrich Heine (c) James Joyce (d) Gertrude Stein

236. All the following books, except one, was written in prison. Which is the exception?
(a) *Don Quixote* by Cervantes (b) *Pilgrim's Progress* by John Bunyon (c) *De Profundis* by Oscar Wilde (d) *Moll Flanders* By Daniel Defoe

237. This poetess loved to smoke cigars. Which of the following?
(a) Elizabeth Barret Browning (b) Alice Meynell (c) Amy Lowell (d) Marianne Moore

238. In his autobiography he wrote about himself that he stood 'in the very first row of second-raters', a view generally endorsed by critics. Who is this author with such books as *Ashenden*, *The Razor's Edge*, and *The Painted Veil*?
(a) John Mortimer (b) Rider Haggard (c) John Steinbeck (d) W. Somerset Maugham

239. Which 'angry young man', a novelist, was for some time a Cambridge don?
(a) Kingsley Amis (b) John Wain (c) John Braine (d) Alan Sillitoe

240. 'An archaeologist is the best husband any woman can have: the older she gets, the more interested he is in her' — spoken from first-hand experience, by whom?
(a) Dame Rebecca West (b) Agatha Christie (c) Monica Dickens (d) Doris Lessing

4

THE INDIAN LITERARY PANORAMA

241. Mr. Morris : How do you do, Mr. Varma. You write in Guj...er...ra...ti?

Mr. Varma : No, in Hindi, India's national language. One hundred and eighty-seven short stories in Hindi. Also four hundred and seventeen poems. In Hindi I am one of the well-known writers.

Mr. Morris : Four hundred and seventeen short stories! My, my, that's something, isn't it? I"d love to see some of them, Mr. Varma.

Mr. Varma : Some I have translated into English, but I am not knowing English very nicely.

Where is this from?
(a) V.S. Naipaul's *An Area of Darkness* (b) Dom Moraes's *My Son's Father* (c) Ved Mehta: *Portrait of India* (d) Nissim Ezekiel: *The Sleepwalkers*

242. The conception, financing, and daily routine of an

English Harem in the middle of the nineteenth century described in the form of the novel' is how one of his books is described by the author, whose novels are again available after a long period of neglect. Who is the author?

(a) G.V. Desani (b) Aubrey Menen (c) Ruskin Bond (d) Varindra Tarzie Vittachi

243. 'Toba Tek Singh', the story of a lunatic waiting to be transferred to the country of his domicile after the partition of India, is perhaps his most famous story, although many of his stories on low life are particularly good. Hailed by some critics as the best short story writer of the subcontinent, he died in 1955. Who is he?

(a) Abdul Hamid Qureishi (b) Kishan Chander (c) K.A. Abbas (d) Saadat Hasan Manto

244. Who is the author of the following books : *The Foreigner, The Apprentice, The Last Labyrinth?*

(a) Nayantara Sahgal (b) Ved Mehta (c) Arun Joshi (d) Dom Moraes

245. Sudhin N. Ghose, a distinguished Indian novelist who wrote in English, won serious critical acclaim in England, although not many in India have read him. Identify his book in the list.

(a) *The Emerald Bower* (b) *The Vermilion Boat* (c) *A Fragrance of Marigold* (d) *The Image in Dust*

246. Who was the first recipient of the Sahitya Akademi

award for English?
(a) Raja Rao (b) R.K. Narayan (c) Mulk Raj Anand
(d) Bhabani Bhattacharya

247. Which, among the following, was Kamala Markandeya's first published novel?
(a) *Some Inner Fury* (b) *Nectar in a Sieve* (c) *A Handful of Rice* (d) *A Silence of Desire*

248. 'A glossary of Anglo-Indian words or phrases and of kindred terms, etymological, historical, geographical and discursive' is how *Hobson-Jobson*, that dictionary of never-ending delights, is described by the authors. Who are they?
(a) Jones and MacNicoll (b) Basham and Roland
(c) Yule and Burnell (d) Jones and Guinson

249. At the age of 19 his first book of verse, appropriately called *A Beginning*, appeared, and next year he received the Hawthornden prize, the youngest poet to do so. Who is he?
(a) Dom Moraes (b) A.K. Ramanujan (c) Nissim Ezekiel (d) Gieve Patel

250. The Sahitya Akademi awards annual prizes for the best writing in Indian languages, one award for each language. How many prizes are given?
(a) 12 (b) 15 (c) 22 (d) 24

251. Amitav Ghosh is among the Indian novelists who have shown great promise and his first novel was

called 'easily the most inventive, brilliant, complex and purposeful first novel produced by an Indian since Salman Rushdie'. Can you identify his novels from this list?
(a) *Ganga* (b) *The Circle of Reason* (c) *A Ship of Fools* (d) *The Shadow Lines*

252. Which, among the following, are collections of Raja Rao's short stories?
(a) *The Cow of the Barricades* (b)*The Cat and Shakespeare* (c) *The Policeman and the Rose* (d) *On the Ganga Ghat*

253. Where is R.K. Narayan's imaginary town Malgudi located?
(a) In Travancore State (b) In Mysore State (c) In Madras Presidency (d) In the Nizam of Hyderabad's territory

254. *Summer in Calcutta* is her first collection of poems, and she is now among the foremost Indian poets writing in English. Who is she?
(a) Tilottama Rajan (b) Gauri Deshpande (c) Amrita Pritam (d) Kamala Das

255. Keki N. Daruwalla, an Indian poet who writes distinguished verse in English, has a collection of short stories among the following books. Identify it.
(a) *Under Orion* (b) *Sword & Abyss* (c) *Apparition in April* (d) *Crossing of Rivers*

256. One of the foremost among Indian cartoonists, he has written a hilarious novel called *Hotel Riviera*. Who is he?
(a) Abu Abraham (b) R.K. Laxman (c) Mario Miranda (d) K. Shankar Pillai

257. The *Siege of Krishnapur*, a novel about the Indian mutiny, was written by
(a) R.K. Narayan (b) John Masters (c) Manohar Malgonkar (d) J.G. Farrell

258. In these days of mushrooming awards, the recipients seem quite happy to receive any; some of them, however, are mercenary enough to find out how much cash the awards dole out. What is the cash down value of the Sahitya Akademi annual awards?
(a) Rs 5000 + unsaleable items (b) Rs 15000 + ditto
(c) Rs 20000 + ditto (d) Rs 25000 + ditto

259. *The Village, Across the Black Waters, The Sword and the Sickle,* and *The Private Life of an Indian Prince* were all written by the same person. Who?
(a) Ruth Prawer Jhabvala (b) R.K. Narayan (c) Aubrey Menen (d) Mulk Raj Anand

260. Who was the founder of the Bharatiya Jnanpith?
(a) G.D. Birla (b) C. Rajagopalachari (c) Sahu S.P. Jain (d) K.M. Munshi

261. Satyajit Ray, the foremost filmmaker of India, is further well known in the field of Bengali literature. In which genre has he made his name?
(a) Lyric poetry (b) Drama (c) Detective fiction (d) Comic fiction

262. Raja Rao is deeply attached to Banaras and the Ganga. Which, among the following books, repeatedly refer to Ganga?
(a) *The Serpent and the Rope* (b) *The Chessmaster and His Moves* (c) *On the Ganga Ghat* (d) *Kanthapura*

263. Ascribe to each author her novels, correctly.
1. Ruth Prawer Jhabvala (a) *Clear Light of Day*
2. Kamala Markandeya (b) *The Day in Shadow*
3. Anita Desai (c) *Heat and Dust* 4. Nayantara Sahgal
(d) *The Nowhere Man*

264. *Sacontala, or the Fatal Ring : an Indian Drama* was published in 1789, and this English translation brought Kalidasa to the notice of the European scholars. Who was the translator?
(a) J. Fergusson (b) H.H. Wilson (c) William Jones (d) E.B. Cowell

265. One of the greatest of Tamil epics is *Silappadikaram* (The Bejewelled Anklet). Who wrote it?
(a) Kamban (b) Sattanar (c) Ilango Adigal (d) Anonymous

266. *A Bend in the River* (1979) is a novel written by

(a) V.S. Naipaul (b) Manohar Malgonkar (c) R.K. Narayan (d) Raja Rao

267. In how many Books or Sections is the *Mahabharata* completed?
(a) 12 (b) 14 (c) 16 (d) 18

268. Correctly match the works with their authors.
1. *Kathasaritsagara* (a) Banabhatta 2. *Geetagovindam* (b) Dandi 3. *Kadambari* (c) Somadeva 4. *Dasakumara-charit* (d) Jayadeva

269. Who wrote *Ramcharitmanas* (the holy lake of the acts of Rama)?
(a) Keshavadas (b) Govindswami (c) Surdas (d) Tulsidas

270. Which of the following were written by Kalidasa?
(a) *Kiratarjuniya* (b) *Mudrarakshasa* (c) *Ritusamhara* (d) *Kadambari*

271. Match the authors with their works.
1. Bana (a) *Rajatarangini* 2. Bilhana (b) *Mudra-rakshasam* 3. Kalhana (c) *Harsacharita* 4. Visakhadatta (d) *Chaurapanchashika*

272. To whom is the original *Mahabharata* ascribed?
(a) Kalidasa (b) Bhavabhuti (c) The Sage Vyasa (d) Sudraka

273. When was the *Ramayana* traditionally composed?

(a) Ninth century B.C. (b) Fifth century B.C.
(c) Third century B.C. (d) A.D. 200

274. The *Ramayanam* is regarded as one of the national
epics of the Tamil people. Who wrote it?
(a) Avvaiyar (b) Kamban (c) Tirukkadavur
(d) Ilango Adigal

275. Who is the original author of the *Ramayana*?
(a) Krittibas Ojha (b) Valmiki (c) Tulsidas
(d) Ramanand Sagar

276. In how many Books or Cantos is the *Bhagavad Gita*
completed?
(a) 10 (b) 14 (c) 18 (d) 19

277. Which among the following films by Satyajit Ray is
based on Tagore?
(a) *The Unvanquished* (b) *Two Daughters* (originally
Three Daughters) (c) *The Middleman* (d) *Distant
Thunder*

278. The earliest surviving Sanskrit poetry is
Buddhacharita, first century A.D. Who is the author?
(a) Sandhyakar (b) Banabhatta (c) Asvaghosa
(d) Somadeva

279. In which language did the Vaishnava poet
Vidyapati write?
(a) Hindi (b) Medieval Bengali (c) Brajabhasa (d)
Maithili

280. Of the following dates, two mark the beginning of the country's major literary awards, viz., Sahitya Akademi Awards and Bharatiya Jnanpith Awards. Choose correctly.
(a) 1953 (b) 1955 (c) 1961 (d) 1965

281. A Hindi poet won both the Jnanpith and Sahitya Akademi awards in recent times. His first published work was *Uchchabas*. Who is he?
(a) Sachchidanand Hiranand Vatsyayan Ajneya
(b) Sumitranandan Panth (c) Maithilisharan Gupta
(d) Jayshankar Prasad

282. Here are four devotional poets from different parts of India. Relate them correctly.
1. Namadev (a) Bihar 2. Shankardev (b) Maharashtra 3. Vidyapati (c) Assam 4. Purandardas (d) Karnataka

283. One of the titles of the following novels of R.K. Narayan is erroneous. Which?
(a) *Mr. Sampath* (b) *The Guide* (c) *Waiting for Mahatma Gandhi* (d) *The Bachelor of Arts*

284. The year Mulk Raj Anand's *Untouchable* was published, 1935, saw the literary debut of an Indian novelist, R.K. Narayan. Which was the book?
(a) *TheBachelor of Arts* (b) *Malgudi Days* (c) *The Man-eater of Malgudi* (d) *Swami and Friends*

285. Many critics regard this as the best novel written on

the partition of India. Yet this novel, which deals with the partition sorrows of the people of Punjab was removed from the syllabus of Punjab University on the grounds of 'obscenity'. Which is it?

(a) *Punjab Century* (b) *Dark Night in Punjab* (c) *Tamas* (d) *Azadi*

286. Satyajit Ray's Apu trilogy is based on two books by a Bengali novelist. Who is he?
(a) Rabindranath Tagore (b) Manik Bandyopadhyay (c) Bimal Mitra (d) Bibhutibhusan Bandyopadhyay

287. Can you identify the novelist from the following books (the most well-known novel is not included, naturally): *The Coffer Dams, The Nowhere Man, Two Virgins,* and *The Golden Honeycomb.*
(a) Bhabani Bhattacharya (b) Anita Desai (c) Kamala Markandeya (d) Manohar Malgonkar

288. There are several good novels on the partition of India and the communal riots that followed. Which novel of Malgonkar on the subject appears on this list?
(a) *Four Months of Forty-seven* (b) *Distant Dream* (c) *Distant Thunder* (d) *A Bend in the Ganges*

289. Which, among the following, is Khushwant Singh's first published book?
(a) *A History of the Sikhs* (b) *Train to Pakistan* (c) *The*

Mark of Vishnu and Other Stories (d) *Many Moods Many Faces*

290. Can you identify Premchand's novels on the list?
(a) *Godaan* (b) *Parakh* (c) *Sanyasi* (d) *Gaban*

291. Ever since the Sahitya Akademi awards were started, most languages missed the award for a year or more. Some have been fortunate though; since awards were instituted, there has not been a missing year. Which are the lucky ones?
(a) Rajasthani (b) Hindi (c) Konkani (d) Nepali

292. *Bande Mataram* used to be a much-sung patriotic song in the days of India's struggle for independence, and was proposed as the national anthem after India's independence. Who wrote it?
(a) Mahamahopadhyay Bidhu Sekhar Shastri
(b) Sarojini Naidu (c) Bankim Chandra Chatterji
(d) None of the above. The song occurs in the *Rigveda*

293. When this author went to England for the first time at the age of 57, after having absorbed English culture all his literate life, a critic called it the consummation of a long love affair. Identify the author and the book.
(a) Nirad C. Chaudhuri : *A Passage to England*
(b) R.K. Narayan : *My Dateless Diary* (c) *Around the World with Khushwant Singh* (d) Rabindranath Tagore : *Letters from Europe*

294. Who wrote India's national anthem *Jana-gana-mana-adhinayaka jaya he*?
(a) Gopal Krishna Gokhale (b) Rabindranath Tagore (c) Mahatma Gandhi (d) Dadabhai Naoroji

295. 'Friends,
    our dear sister
    is departing for foreign
    in two three days...'
    Thus begins a hilarious poem written in 'Indian English'. Who wrote it?
    (a) Keki N. Daruwalla (b) Shiv K. Kumar (c) Nissim Ezekiel (d) Gieve Patel

296. In 1976 an important anthology of present-day Indian poets who write in English was published under the name *Ten Twentieth-Century Indian Poets*. Who was the editor?
    (a) R. Parthasarathy (b) Shiv K. Kumar (c) Saleem Peeradina (d) Gauri Deshpande

297. What is the Jnanpith award for?
    (a) The best writer in any particular Indian language (chosen by rotation) for the current year.
    (b) The best book in Hindi literature for the last fifteen years. (c) The best creative writing by any Indian in any of the Indian languages in the last twenty years. (d) The best literary work in any language which helps national integration.

298. When was the first Jnanpith award presented?

(a) 1949 (b) 1956 (c) 1960 (d) 1965

299. Who was the recipient of the first Bharatiya Jnanpith Award?
(a) Tarashankar Banerjee (Bengali) (b) Umasanker Joshi (Gujarati) (c) Sumitranandan Panth (Hindi) (d) G. Shankara Kurup (Malayalam)

300. Match the following authors with the languages in which they write.
1. M.K. Binodini Devi (a) Malayalam 2. K. Ayyappa Paniker (b) Manipuri 3. Ka. Naa. Subramanyam (c) Maithili 4. Lili Ray (d) Tamil

301. Identify Phaniswar Nath Renu's novel among the following:
(a) *Kayakalpa* (b) *Sanyasi* (c) *Maila Anchal* (d) *Premashram*

302. One of Assam's foremost literary figures, he received both the Sahitya Akademi and Jnanpith awards. Who is he?
(a) Nabakanta Barua (b) Birendra Kumar Bhattacharya (c) Hitesh Deka (d) Chandrakanta Gogoi

303. *The Strange Case of Billy Biswas* is a moving and significant novel about the U.S.-educated Billy and his disappearance into a tribal society. Who is the author?
(a) Mulk Raj Anand (b) C.L. Nahal (c) Arun Joshi

(d) Kishori Charan Das

304. Penguin Books came out with an anthology of Indian writing in English in 1974, called *New Writing in India*. Who edited it?
(a) Nissim Ezekiel (b) A.K. Ramanujan (c) Arun Kolatkar (d) Adil Jussawalla

305. 'The poet, he being neither Muslim nor Hindu in India', a poem about communal hatred begins with this memorable line : 'To be no part of this hate is deprivation'. Who is the poet?
(a) Nissim Ezekiel (b) Adil Jussawalla (c) Gieve Patel (d) K.D. Kartak

306. Can you arrange the following novels of Salman Rushdie in their chronological order?
(a) *Midnight's Children* (b) *Satanic Verses* (c) *Grimus* (d) *Shame*

307. The stories of *Panchatantra*, moral fables, were written to educate a dunce in no time. Who wrote them?
(a) Vishakhadatta (b) Somadeva (c) Vishnu Sharma (d) Bharavi

308. Among the Sahitya Akademi award-winners in English there are some notable omissions, although between 1955 and 1988, no awards could be made on fourteen occasions. Who are the omissions?

(a) Khushwant Singh (b) Manohar Malgonkar
(c) Nirad C. Chaudhuri (d) Nissim Ezekiel

309. 'A *tour de force* of rhyme and reasonableness, *The Golden Gate* does'nt only compellingly advocate life's pleasure, it stylishly contributes another to them', wrote the *Sunday Times* of London. Who wrote the book?
(a) Ranga Rao (b) Shashi Despande (c) Vikram Seth
(d) Aubrey Menen

310. The Sahitya Akademi awards were started in 1955, yet the writing in one language was considered so poor that for the first years, i.e., till 1960, no awards could be made. Which is that language?
(a) Bengali (b) English (c) Kashmiri (d) Punjabi

311. In 1968, the Sahitya Akademi award for Marathi went to *Yugant*, an interpretation of the *Mahabharata*, later translated into English as *Yuganta*. Who was the author?
(a) Saratchandra Muktibodh (b) Indira Sant
(c) Iravati Karve (d) N.G. Kalelkar

312. Exhibit 134 at the Patna Museum is the Yakshi from Didarganj. Who wrote a memorable poem on the Yakshi which has these lines:

'Fairy,
Yakshi, beloved, stone, girl with feather fan,
Carved in dreams for fits of phallic fury,
Purge flesh of desire!

Purge it in pools of fire!'
(a) A.K. Ramanujan (b) P. Lal (c) Pritish Nandi
(d) Shrikant Varma

313. *My Son's Father* is the autobiography of an Indian
poet. Which?
(a) A.K. Ramanujan (b) Dom Moraes (c) Gieve Patel
(d) Nissim Ezekiel

314. Who in his egotistical prayers says
'Confiscate my passport, Lord,
I don't want to go abroad.
Let me find my song
where I belong'?
(a) Arvind Mehrotra (b) Arun Kolatkar (c) Nissim
Ezekiel (d) Gieve Patel

315. Which, among the following, is Raja Rao's latest
book?
(a) *On the Ganga Ghat* (b) *The Policeman and the Rose*
(c) *The Chessmaster and His Moves* (d) *Comrade
Kirillov*

316. 'This poem has earned me the most in copyright
fees', says the poet about this much-anthologized
poem : a few of its lines reading :
'May the sum of evil
balanced in this unreal world
against the sum of good
become diminished by your pain, they said'.
Which is the poem?

(a) 'Haranag' by Keki N. Daruwalla (b) 'Snakes' by A.K. Ramanujan (c) 'The Night of the Scorpion' By Nissim Ezekiel (d) 'Migraine' by Gauri Deshpande

317. Naranappa, Putta, Manjunatha, Shripati, and Manjayya are some of the minor characters in a Kannada novel whose English translation by an eminent poet established its fame as one of the finest Indian novels to be written in the last twenty years. Which novel is it?
(a) *A Time to Die* (b) *The Unchaste* (c) *The Sins of Appu's Mother* (d) *Samskara*

318. Which was Mulk Raj Anand's first published novel?
(a) *Untouchable* (b) *Coolie* (c) *Two Leaves and a Bud* (d) *The Village*

319. Some of the following books are by Khushwant Singh. Identify them.
(a) *A History of the Akalis* (b) *Many Moods Many Faces* (c) *I Shall Not Hear the Nightingale* (d) *Train to Pakistan*

320. Who, among the following, are Jnanpith award winners?
(a) Premendra Mitra (b) A.K. Ramanujan (c) Jayanta Mahapatra (d) P.V. Akilandam

321. Manohar Malgonkar was a professional hunter, a lieutenant colonel in the British Indian army, and a

teaplanter. He also wrote a memorable novel about the Sepoy Mutiny. Which, among the following is it?
(a) *Tantia Topi* (b) *Combat of Shadows* (c) *A Bend in the Ganges* (d) *The Devil's Wind*

322. Jaishankar Prasad made considerable literary reputation by writing an epic. Which is it?
(a) *Bharat Bharati* (b) *Priya Pravas* (c) *Kamayani* (d) *Chidambara*

323. An Indian author was closely associated in the 1930s with T.S. Eliot, Herbert Read, and George Orwell, participating with them in contemporary literary movements and appearing at BBC Third Programmes. Who is he?
(a) Bhabani Bhattacharya (b) K.A. Abbas (c) Mulk Raj Anand (d) Raja Rao

324. Like Raja Rao, there is an Indian writing in English who is fascinated by the Ganga, and has written memorable poems about the river. Who is he?
(a) Keki N. Daruwalla (b) Kamala Das (c) Nissim Ezekiel (d) R. Parthasarathy

325. Of the following names of Bhabani Bhattacharya's books one is slightly miswritten. Tell which.
(a) *He Who Rides a Tiger* (b) *So Many Hungers* (c) *A Dream in Hawaii* (d) *Steel Hawk and Other Stories*

326. In which year was Rabindranath Tagore awarded

the Nobel Prize for literature?
(a) 1906 (b) 1909 (c) 1913 (d) 1921

327. *All about H. Hatterr* is one of the landmarks of Indian fiction in English. Who wrote it?
(a) G.V. Desani (b) R.C. Dutt (c) Anita Desai (d) A.K. Ramanujan

328. In which year was Tagore's *Gitanjali* in English translation first published?
(a) 1905 (b) 1912 (c) 1915 (d) 1921

329. Who is the current President of the Sahitya Akademi?
(a) Mulk Raj Anand (b) R.K. Narayan (c) Birendra Kumar Bhattachryya (d) The Education Secretary, Government of India

330. *Madhushala* is an important contemporary Hindi epic poem, recently published in a revised English translation. Who wrote it?
(a) Shrikant Varma (b) Maithili Sharan Gupta (c) Mahadevi Verma (d) Harivanshrai Bachchan

331. Of the following books, which are not Mulk Raj Anand's?
(a) *Private Life of an Indian Prince* (b) *Across the Black Waters* (c) *The Sickle and the Sword* (d) *Tales from the Punjab*

332. The 1988 Sahitya Akademi award for Urdu went

posthumously to someone who was also eminent in another field. Who is he?

(a) Firaq Gorakhpuri (b) Sheikh Muhammed Abdulla (c) Jan Nisar Akhtar (d) S. Abid Hussain

333. In which scripts were the Ashokan edicts written?
(a) Brahmi (b) Magadhi (c) Sauraseni (d) Kharoshthi

334. Which is the oldest Indian linguistic text?
(a) Panini's *Astadhyayi* (b) Patanjali's *Mahabhasya* (c) Jayaditya and Vamana's *Kasika Vritti* (d) Yaska's *Nirukta*

335. Where is the earliest surviving form of Sanskrit to be found?
(a) *The Rig Veda* (b) *The Mahabharata* (c) *The Sam Veda* (d) *The Mahabhasya* of Patanjali

336. Between which set of dates did Rabindranath Tagore live?
(a) 1889 and 1967 (b) 1830 and 1918 (c) 1861 and 1941 (d) 1850 and 1939

337. Among the following, can you identify Bhabani Bhattacharya's first published book?
(a) *Music for Mohini* (b) *So Many Hungers!* (c) *He who Rides a Tiger* (d) *Shadow from Ladakh*

338. There is only one foreign Honorary Fellow at the Sahitya Akademi, and he is a distinguished poet.

Can you name him?
(a) Philip Larkin (b) Joseph Brodsky (c) Leopold Sedar Senghor (d) Gunter Grass

339. The two-thousand-year-old epic, the *Mahabharata*, has now been told in twentieth-century terms in a clever take-off, called 'an Iliad of Independent India'. Which is the book?
(a) *The Great Indian Novel* (b) *A Bhishma of Our Times* (c) *India Rediscovered* (d) *Bharat India Hindustan*

340. Delightful short stories about small towns and villages, the adolescent experience, and the hills with which the author has been in love all his life-only inadequately express the distinction of this author. His *Room on the Roof*, written at the age of 17 won a prestigious British literary award. Can you identify any of his books from the following?
(a) *The Night Train of Deoli and Other Stories* (b) *The Room at the Top* (c) *Time Must Have a Stop* (d) *The Leopard of Pipalnagar*

341. *Storm in Chandigarh* is a novel about the bone of contention between the states of Punjab and Haryana, rousing passions no less than at the time of partition of the country. Who is the author?
(a) Anita Desai (b) Manohar Malgonkar (c) Nayantara Sahgal (d) Khushwant Singh

342. Which contemporary Indian dramatist wrote *Tughlaq*, a successful stage play?

(a) Vijay Tendulkar (b) Girish Karnad (c) Ba‹
Sirkar (d) Mohan Rakesh

5

GREEK AND LATIN HEAVYWEIGHTS

343. In Greek mythology, this king, in retaliation for his brother's seduction of his wife, killed three of his nephews and served them to his brother in a feast. The brother laid a curse on the murderer's family—whose effects are delineated in a number of Greek tragedies. Who is the king?
(a) Thyestes (b) Atreus (c) Agamemnon (d) Menelaus

344. Daughter of Minos and Pasiphaci, and wife of Theseus, she fell in love with her stepson. Rejected, she accused him of rape and hanged herself. Who is this lady?
(a) Antiope (b) Persephone (c) Ariadne (d) Phaedra

345. Cassandra, endowed with prophetic powers, was the daughter of
(a) Agamemnon and Clytemnestra (b) Odysseus and Penelope (c) Priam and Hecuba (d) Hector and Andromache

346. Clytemnestra was not the mother of one of the following:
(a) Orestes (b) Oedipus (c) Electra (d) Iphigenia

347. Which among the following plays is by Aeschylus?
(a) *Antigone* (b) *Electra* (c) *Oedipus at Colonus*
(d) *The Seven against Thebes*

348. Match the authors with their works.
1. Lucan (a) *Amphitryon* 2. Ovid (b) *Pharsalia*
3. Seneca (c) *Amores* 4. Plautus (d) *Medea*

349. Match the authors with their plays.
1. Aeschylus (a) *Lysistrata* 2. Aristophanes
(b) *Antigone* 3. Euripides (c) *Eumenides* 4. Sophocles
(d) *Alcestis*

350. Match the authors with the dates and arrange in order of seniority.
1. Sophocles (a) 480-406 B.C. 2. Euripides (b) 496-406 B.C. 3. Aristophanes (c) 525-456 B.C.
4. Aeschylus (d) *c* 448-380 B.C.

351. A very long Latin poem tells more than two hundred stories. They have one thing in common. They are all tales of magic changes of shape. Which poem is it?
(a) *Pharsalia* (b) *Metamorphoses* (c) *Silvae* (d) *Georgics*

352. Which, among the following gods and goddesses, take sides in the Trojan war in *Iliad*?

(a) Athena (b) Aphrodite (c) Zeus (d) Hera

353. Who was the tutor of Alexander the great?
(a) Plato (b) Aristotle (c) Socrates (d) Xenophon

354. A great Stoic philosopher, tutor to young Nero, and later by Nero's command forced to commit suicide, his influence on Elizabethan tragedy was considerable. Who is he?
(a) Plautus (b) Seneca (c) Terence (d) Lucan

355. Tennyson's 'Ulysses' was based on an episode described in
(a) Homer's *Odyssey* (b) Vergil's *Aeneid* (c) Pliny's *Natural History* (d) Dante's *Inferno*

356. W.H. Auden wrote 'Homage to Clio'. Which subject is she the Muse of?
(a) Poetry (b) History (c) Dancing (d) Learning

357. *Metamorphoses* or *The Golden Ass* is originally a hilariously comic novel written in Latin. Who is the author?
(a) Boccaccio (b) Apuleius (c) St. Thomas Aquinas (d) Horace

358. Aeschylus's *Oresteia* comprises all but one of the following plays. Which is the exception?
(a) *Agamemnon* (b) *Oedipus Rex* (c) *Choephoroe* (d) *Euminides*

359. The Peloponnesian war was fought between rival alliances led by Athens and Sparta, and broke out in 431 B.C. Who wrote a memorable history of it?
(a) Livy (b) Plutarch (c) Thucydides (d) Herodotus

360. In Greek mythology, who is the god of travellers, luck, music, eloquence, commerce, young men, cheats, and thieves?
(a) Hermes (b) Zeus (c) Rhea (d) Cronos

361. Pallas Athena, daughter of Zeus, was the goddess of
(a) Music (b) Dramatic arts (c) War (d) Poetry

362. The Trojan War was also the cause of acute rivalry between gods. Can you identify from the list the gods and goddesses who supported the Greeks?
(a) Hera (b) Poseidon (c) Athena (d) Aphrodite

363. So Oedipus kills his father and marries Jocasta, who is his mother. When he discovers the truth, he blinds himself. What does Jocasta do?
(a) Commits Suicide (b) Flees the country (c) Becomes insane (d) Does nothing and goes on living as the Queen of Thebes

364. The truly capable ruler must combine the qualities of the lion and the fox, the bravery of one and the craftiness of the other — says a famous book on statecraft. Whose book is it?
(a) Plato in *Republic* (b) Rousseau in *Social Contract*

(c) Machiavelli in *The Prince* (d) Hitler in *Mein Kampf*

365. What is common between Hector, Paris, Troilus, and Cassandra?
(a) They were all crossed in love (b) They all belonged to the Greek camp in the Trojan war (c) They were all children of King Priam and Queen Hecuba (d) They were all killed in the Trojan war

366. Plutarch's *Lives* was actually called *Parallel Lives*. This was because Plutarch
(a) compared the actual lives of his subjects with those found in myths (b) compared the lives of the virtuous with those of the wicked (c) wrote both about Romans and Greeks, comparing each to the other (d) drew comparisons in each life between the glories of the past and the decay of the present.

367. Match the legendary lovers correctly.
1. Abelard (a) Cressida 2. Leander (b) Eurydice 3. Diomedes (c) Heloise 4. Orpheus (d) Hero

368. Plato, the Greek philosopher, lived between
(a) *c*. 627 — *c*. 538 B.C. (b) *c*. 428 — *c*. 348 B.C. (c) *c*. A.D. 238 — 298 (d) *c*. A.D. 528 — 578

369. Atalanta of Greek mythology was a
(a) poetess (b) unfaithful wife (c) murderess (d) huntress

370. When were *The Iliad* and *The Odyssey* composed?
(a) Before 700 B.C. (b) Before 1100 B.C. (c) After A.D. 200 (d) After A.D. 500

371. This historian wrote a History of Rome in 142 books, only 35 of which survive. Who is he?
(a) Livy (b) Pliny (c) Sallust (d) Tacitus

372. Which is the only surviving Latin novel?
(a) Seneca the Younger's *Phoenissae* (b) Plautus's *Vidularia* (c) Macrobius's *Saturnalia* (d) Apuleius's *The Golden Ass*

373. Which is the Sophoclean play among the following?
(a) *Medea* (b) *Philoctetes* (c) *Alcestis* (d) *Hippolytus*

374. When was Parthenon, the temple of Athena on the Acropolis in Athens, built?
(a) Seventh century B.C. (b) Fifth century B.C. (c) A.D. 272 — 93 (d) A.D. 398 — 410

375. He loved faithless Lesbia and addressed to her gay, tender, and obscenely derisive poems. Identify the poet.
(a) Lucan (b) Ovid (c) Catullus (d) Seneca

376. Who was the first husband of Helen of Troy?
(a) Paris (b) Agamemnon (c) Achilles (d) Menelaus

377. He married a nymph, and when she died he descended to Hades and was allowed to return

with her on condition that he would not look back at her. As you can guess, he did, and lost her forever. Whose story is this?
(a) Apollo and Daphne (b) Jason and Medea (c) Perseus and Andromeda (d) Orpheus and Eurydice

378. 'I Tiresias, old man with wrinkled dugs
Perceived the scene, and foretold the rest —'
This blind soothsayer who had been changed into a woman for a short time, plays an important part in Greek tragedies. Which of the following?
(a) *Oedipus the King* (b) *Seven against Thebes* (c) *Euminides* (d) *Alcestis*

379. Who was the creator of the Sculptures of Parthenon, Athens?
(a) Callicrates (b) Praxiteles (c) Hephaestus (d) Phidias

380. Who were the Sirens in the Greek myths?
(a) Sisters who lured newcomers into their islands and turned them to sheep (b) Nymphs whose songs put men to sleep, when they devoured them (c) Nymphs whose songs lured sailors to shipwreck on the rocky coast where they lived (d) Sisters whose songs lured sailors to their island and made them forget their past lives

381. Who is the author of *Lives of the Caesars*?
(a) Livy (b) Cicero (c) Plutarch (d) Suetonius

6

BEARD THE BARD

382. Who before his death makes this memorable pun in a play by Shakespeare, 'Ask for me tomorrow and you shall find me a grave man'?
(a) Laertes (b) Cassio (c) Mercutio (d) Hotspur

383. 'Lay her i' the earth;
And from her fair and unpolluted flesh
May violets spring!'
— Who are these lines about?
(a) Desdemona (b) Ophelia (c) Cordelia (d) Helena

384. 'Men must endure
their going hence, even as their coming hither:
Ripeness is all.'
Who says this in which Shakespearean play?
(a) Edgar in *King Lear* (b) Brutus in *Julius Caesar*
(c) Horatio in *Hamlet* (d) Enobarbus in *Antony and Cleopatra*

385. Who is the Shakespearean character who 'apprehends death no more dreadfully but as a

drunken sleep; careless, reckless, and fearless of what's past, present, or to come'?
(a) One of the gravediggers in *Hamlet* (b) Bernardine in *Measure for Measure* (c) Antony in *Antony and Cleopatra* (d) Mercutio in *Romeo and Juliet*

386. 'But thought's the slave of life, and life time's fool;
And time, that makes survey of all the world,
Must have a stop.'
Who says this and where?
(a) Macbeth in *Macbeth* (b) Iago in *Othello* (c) Hotspur in *Henry IV* (d) Hamlet in *Hamlet*

387. 'Nothing in his life
Became him like the leaving it…'
Who is the speaker and who is spoken about?
(a) Enobarbus on Antony (b) Horatio on Hamlet (c) Malcolm on the Thane of Cawdor (d) Lucilius on Brutus

388. In which Shakespearean play does the following occur?
'The bright day is done,
And we are for the dark.'
(a) *Hamlet* (b) *Measure for Measure* (c) *King Lear* (d) *Antony and Cleopatra*

389. 'Age cannot wither her, nor custom stale
Her infinite variety. Other women cloy
The appetites they feed, but she makes hungry

Where most she satisfies...'
This tribute to Cleopatra is paid by a cynic. Who ?
(a) Ventidius (b) Enobarbus (c) Octavius Caesar
(d) Charmian

390. 'As flies to wanton boys, are we to the gods;
They kill us for their sport.'
— Whose pessimistic utterance is this?
(a) Gloucestor in *King Lear* (b) King Lear in *King Lear*
(c) Othello in *Othello* (d) Troilus in *Troilus and
Cressida*

391. 'There is a tide in the affairs of women,
Which, taken at the flood, leads — God knows
where.'
This is Byron's parody of Shakespeare. In which
play do the original lines occur?
(a) *Coriolanus* (b) *Richard III* (c) *Julius Caesar*
(d) *Macbeth*

392. 'Many a good hanging prevents a bad marriage.' In
which play of Shakespeare does this occur?
(a) *As You Like It* (b) *Much Ado About Nothing* (c) *The
Taming of the Shrew* (d) *Twelfth Night*

393. Shakespeare's *King Lear* was banned in England in
1788 (ban lifted in 1820) because it was thought to
reflect on a King's insanity. Who was the king?
(a) George III (b) James II (c) Edward IV (d) Edward
III

394. Who were the editors of the first collection of Shakespeare's plays, The First Folio?
(a) Ben Jonson and Michael Drayton (b) John Middleton and Cyril Tourneur (c) John Heminge and Henry Condell (d) Francis Beaumont and John Fletcher

395. When was the first complete collection of Shakespeare's plays, known as the First Folio, published?
(a) 1613 (b) 1616 (c) 1623 (d) 1632

396. How many plays were included in the first standard edition of Shakespeare's plays — an edition now accepted as complete, except for *Pericles*, parts of which Shakespeare is judged to have written?
(a) 26 (b) 36 (c) 46 (d) 29

397. Of the following, who has been proposed most often as the real author of Shakespeare's plays?
(a) Christopher Marlowe (b) Francis Bacon (c) Edward de Vere, Earl of Oxford (d) Sir Philip Sidney

398. Saxo Grammaticus, thirteenth century Danish historian, provided Shakepeare with the story of a much-filmed, much-acted play. Which is it?
(a) *Hamlet* (b) *Macbeth* (c) *King Lear* (d) *As You Like It*

399. Of Shakespeare one of his contemporaries said that

he had small Latin and less Greek. Who was this contemporary?
(a) Christopher Marlowe (b) Ben Jonson (c) Robert Greene (d) John Lyly

400. What is Shakespeare's date of birth?
(a) 1664 (b) 1590 (c) 1536 (d) 1564

401. And when did Shakespeare die?
(a) 1616 (b) 1623 (c) 1613 (d) 1626

402. The first complete collection of Shakespeare's plays (1623) has survived bibliographical scrutiny. Only another play has been added to its 36, although it is not completely Shakespearean. Which is it?
(a) *Sir Thomas More* (b) *Henry VIII* (c) *Pericles* (d) *Two Noble Kinsmen*

403. Of the 1200 copies of the first complete collection of Shakespeare's plays, the First Folio, how many have survived?
(a) None (b) Around 60 (c) Around 570 (d) Around 230

404. The First Folio, the first complete collection of Shakespeare's plays, comprised published and unpublished works. How many of each?
(a) 18 plus 18 (b) 26 published, 10 unpublished (c) 28 published, 8 unpublished (d) 16 published, 20 unpublished

405. In which play of Shakespeare does Sir Andrew Aguecheek play a part?
(a) *Cymbeline* (b) *Twelfth Night* (c) *Merry Wives of Windsor* (d) *King Henry IV, Part I*

406. A young nobleman is ordered by the king to marry a girl he knows, but does not love. After the wedding, however, the young man promptly leaves her, without consummating the marriage, telling her that he will acknowledge her as wife only when she can get the ring from his finger, and — is with child by him. The young woman achieves both the feats by trickery and is accepted by her husband. Which amazing play has this plot?
(a) *All's Well That Ends Well* (b) *A Trick to Catch the Old One* (c) *Measure for Measure* (d) *The Maid's Tragedy*

407. Antigonus, husband of Paulina, has a remarkable death, indicated by the stage direction *'Exit, pursued by a bear'*. In which play by Shakespeare does this happen?
(a) *Cymbeline* (b) *All's Well That Ends Well* (c) *Pericles* (d) *The Winter's Tale*

408. One of the following Shakespearean Antonios is inauthentic. Which?
(a) Bassanio's friend (b) Leonato's brother (c) Prospero's usurping brother (d) Cleopatra's lover

409. The Spanish Armada of 1588 was all sound and fury and was easily dispersed, but gave Shakespeare a name for a braggart, Don Armado. In which play does he brag?
(a) *Love's Labour Lost* (b) *Much Ado about Nothing*
(c) *Twefth Night* (d) *The Taming of the Shrew*

410. Originally one of the three Magi, Balthazar is also the name of a Shakespearean character. In which play does he appear?
(a)*Much Ado about Nothing* (b)*Measure for Measure*
(c) *The Merchant of Venice* (d) *The Winter's Tale*

411. In *Hamlet*, Ophelia, now mad, distributes various flowers to those present. She does not give one of the following flowers. Which?
(a) Rosemary (b) Pansies (c) Columbines (d) Violets

412. Elsinore in Denmark is the scene of a Shakespearean play. Which?
(a) *King Lear* (b) *Hamlet* (c) *Titus Andronicus*
(d) *Coriolanus*

413. 'The Sonnets beginning CXXVII to his mistress are worse than a puzzle-peg. They are abominably harsh, obscure and worthless.' Who made this pronouncement on Shakespeare's *Sonnets*?
(a) Dr Johnson (b) Wordsworth (c) Coleridge
(d) F.R. Leavis

414. Match the characters with the plays:

1. Artemidorus (a) *Macbeth*   2. Fleance (b) *Julius Caesar* 3. Bernardo (c) *Othello* 4. Bianca (d) *Hamlet*

415. Of the plays mentioned below, one was not written by Shakespeare. Which?
(a) *Two Noble Kinsmen* (b) *The Merry Wives of Windsor* (c) *Two Gentlemen of Verona* (d) *The Comedy of Errors*

416. Where does the action of Shakespeare's *Coriolanus* take place?
(a) Venice (b) Sparta (c) Rome (d) Athens

417. Where does the action of Shakespeare's *Measure for Measure* lie?
(a) Venice (b) Verona (c) Vienna (d) Messina

418. In which play of Shakespeare does Adam appear?
(a) *Merry Wives of Windsor* (b) *As You Like It* (c) *Twelfth Night* (d) *Tempest*

419. Eliot's 'A game of chess ends with repeated good nights to ladies'. Which Shakespearean play does it echo?
(a) *Màcbeth* (b) *King Lear* (c) *Othello* (d) *Hamlet*

420. A famous character in Shakespeare's plays used to spend much of his time at this tavern. Which?
(a) The Mitre (rhymes with fighter) Tavern(b) The White Heart Inn (c) The Devil Tavern (d) The Boar's Head Inn

421. In which Shakespearean play does Curan appear?
(a) *Macbeth* (b) *Othello* (c) *King Lear* (d) *Coriolanus*

422. Match the characters with the plays:
1. Benvolio (a) *Romeo and Juliet* 2. Virgilia (b) *Antony and Cleopatra* 3. Mardian (c) *Cymbeline* 4. Iachimo (d) *Coriolanus*

423. The character Antonio appears in five of Shakespeare's plays, but only in three of the following. Which is the exception?
(a) *The Merchant of Venice* (b) *Much Ado About Nothing* (c) *The Tempest* (d) *The Taming of the Shrew*

424. How much could Shakespeare have earned from *Hamlet*?
(a) £ 5 (b) 12s. 6d. (c) £ 195 (d) £ 39,6,500,000

7

DRAMATISTS AND THEIR PERSONAE

425. 'In that moment it burst upon me that I had been living here these eight years with a strange man, and had borne him three children.' In which play do these lines occur and who speaks them?
(a) Ann, in Shaw's *Man and Superman* (b) Nora, in Ibsen's *Doll's House* (c) Vivie, in Shaw's *Mrs. Warren's Profession* (d) Alison, in John Osborne's *Look Back in Anger*

426. This on the role of the artist in society: 'My dear Tristan, to be an artist *at all* is like living in Switzerland during a world war'. Which modern dramatist has this in his dialogue?
(a) Tom Stoppard (b) Peter Shaffer (c) Trevor Morris (d) Samuel Beckett

427. A modern dramatist said this in explanation of his craft: 'Life is very nice, but it lacks form. It's the aim of art to give it some.' Which dramatist?
(a) Jean Anouilh (b) Bertolt Brecht (c) Harold Pinter (d) Luigi Pirandello

428. 'Cover her face; mine eyes dazzle: She died young.'—Who is the speaker and who is the object?
(a) Hamlet, on Ophelia (b) Othello, on Desdemona (c) Ferdinand, on the Duchess of Malfi (d) Lear, on Cordelia

429. 'It is a woman's business to get married as soon as possible, and a man's to keep unmarried as long as he can.' Where is this said?
(a) John Osborne's *Look Back in Anger* (b) Bernard Shaw's *Man and Superman* (c) William Congreve's *The Way of the World* (d) Sheridan's *The Rivals*

430. A group of dramatists and poets, Shakespeare's contemporaries, were engaged in free-thinking philosophical debate, and dabbled in such things as alchemy and the occult. They were given the name 'School of Night'. Who, among the following, belonged to it?
(a) William Shakespeare (b) Robert Greene (c) Christopher Marlowe (d) George Chapman

431. Racine replaced Corneille as France's leading tragedian and earned the enmity of the latter's admirers, who included Moliere. Which play of Racine's brought about this change in the No. 1 position?
(a) *Andromaque* (b) *Berenice* (c) *Iphigenie en Aulide* (d) *Phedre*

432. What is a Passion Play?

(a) A play about love and sex (b) A play about man's intense love for God (c) A play about the suffering, death and resurrection of Jesus (d) A play from the New Testament showing Jesus's love for man.

433. *The Admirable Crichton* (1902) has been an ever-popular play on the stage. Who wrote it?
(a) W.S. Gilbert (b) James Barrie (c) Arthur Sullivan (d) James Stephens

434. Francis Beaumont and John Fletcher collaborated in so many plays that it is difficult to ascribe individual authorship to plays associated with either. Which of the following plays is now generally ascribed to Beaumont alone?
(a) *Philaster* (b) *A Maid's Tragedy* (c) *The Knight of the Burning Pestle* (d) *A King and No King*

435. The subject of Thomas Becket's martyrdom has been treated dramatically by several writers. Who, among the following?
(a) Tennyson (b) John Arden (c) T.S. Eliot (d) Jean Anouilh

436. The Seven Years War (1756-63) is the background of one of Bertolt Brecht's plays. Which?
(a) *The Good Woman of Setzuan* (b) *Mother Courage* (c) *Caucasian Chalk Circle* (d) *The Measures Taken*

437. In whose play does this exclamation occur: 'Gracious me! I have been talking prose for the last

forty years and have never known it'?
(a) Moliere (b) Racine (c) Sartre (d) Ibsen

438. Identify the plays associated with the Theatre of the Absurd in the following list.
(a) *The Bald Prima Donna* (b) *The Blacks* (c) *Who's Afraid of Virginia Woolf?* (d) *The Rose Tattoo*

439. The following are the dates between which these four dramatists lived. Match the names with the dates.
1. Shakespeare (a) 1572/3 and 1637 2. Marlowe (b) 1580 and 1627 3. Ben Jonson (c) 1564 and 1593 (d) Middleton (d) 1564 and 1616

440. The Theatre of the Absurd conceives the world as fundamentally mysterious and indecipherable; recognition of this is associated with feelings of loss, purposelessness, and bewilderment. Who, among the following, are associated with this theatre?
(a) Edward Albee (b) Eugene Ionesco (c) Henrik Ibsen (d) Samuel Beckett

441. *Eastward Hoe* (1605) was a comedy written by Jonson, Chapman, and Marston. A couple of years later another comedy appeared, called *Westward Hoe.* Who were the authors?
(a) Middleton and Massinger (b) Webster and Dekker (c) Middleton and Chapman (d) Chapman and Dekker

442. Nicholas Udall (1505-56) is regarded as having

written the first complete comedy in English. Which is it?

(a) *Gammer Gurtons Needle* (b) *Ralph Roister Doister*
(c) *Endimion* (d) *Friar Bacon and Friar Bungay*

443. Perhaps the longest title (*perhaps,* because we have not checked with the *Guinness Book of Records*) of a play is *The Persecution and Assassination of Jean Paul Marat as Performed by the Inmates of the Asylum of Charenton Under the Direction of the Marquis de Sade* (1964). What is the name of the playwright?

(a) Bertolt Brecht (b) Henri de Montherlant
(c) Marguerite Duras (d) Peter Weiss

444. Who is the author of the following plays (names in English translation): *Thieves' Carnival, Antigone, Ring Round the Moon,* and *Becket; or, the Honour of God?*

(a) Jean Genet (b) Jean Giradoux (c) Jean Anouilh
(d) Jean-Paul Sartre

445. In which play do the trio of gulls, viz., Dapper, Drugger, and Kastril make an appearance?

(a) *The Honest Whore* (b) *The Alchemist* (c) *A Trick to Catch the Old One* (d) *The Malcontent*

446. *The Seagull,* one of his earlier plays, flopped miserably when it was first put up. However, when it was produced at the Moscow Art Theatre, one of whose founders was Stanislavsky, it was a triumph. Who is the playwright?

(a) Ivan Bunin (b) Nikolai Gogol (c) Anton Chekhov

(d) Maxim Gorky

447. Who is the character in a seventeenth century drama who goes on dancing as she hears the news of three deaths, but finally drops dead?
(a) Phyllida (b) Penthea (c) Calantha (d) Arethusa

448. 'Sweet Helen, make me immortal with a kiss.' Whose supplication is this?
(a) Menelaus (b) Paris (c) Dr. Faustus (d) Mephistopheles

449. A hermaphrodite is an animal (or plant) with both male and female reproductive systems. In *Volpone* there is one. Who?
(a) Nano (b) Castrone (c) Corvino (d) Androgyno

450. This American playwright was well known for his drama of social protest, and his *Waiting for Lefty* (1935) was widely performed. Who is he?
(a) Eugene O' Neill (b) Tennesse Williams (c) Clifford Odets (d) Arthur Miller

451. Who wrote *Orpheus Descending, The Rose Tattoo, Camino Real,* and *Suddenly Last Summer*?
(a) Arthur Miller (b) Eugene O' Neill (c) Tennesse Williams (d) Clifford Odets

452. *The School for Scandal* is a society comedy in which characters like Lady Teazle, Sir Benjamin Backbite and Lady Sneerwell apear. Who wrote it?

(a) R.B. Sheridan (b) William Congreve (c) George Etheredge (d) Oscar Wilde

453. *Desire under the Elms* is a powerful play made into a film. Which American dramatist wrote it?
(a) Arthur Miller (b) Tennesse Williams (c) Eugene O' Neill (d) Thornton Wilder

454. The Ibsen play put up in London in 1880 was largely ignored. Its translator was William Archer, who did many subsequent translations of Ibsen. Which was the play?
(a) *The Pillars of Society* (b) *An Enemy of the People* (c) *A Doll's House* (d) *Peer Gynt*

455. Posthumous son of a clegryman, bricklayer, soldier, player in a strolling company, convicted for sedition and slander, in danger of being hanged, as also on another occasion of having his nose and ears slit, this man nevertheless became one of the most important English dramatists of all time. Who is he?
(a) Christopher Marlowe (b) Robert Greene (c) Ben Jonson (d) George Chapman

456. Harley Granville-Barker, an eminent theatre producer and Shakespearean critic, established the reputation of some twentieth century dramatists. Whose, among the following?
(a) Sir Arthur Pinero (b) George Bernard Shaw (c) John Galsworthy (d) James Barrie

457. Who wrote *A Taste of Honey,* hailed as a landmark in the school of 'Kitchen Sink' realism?
(a) John Osborne (b) Arnold Wesker (c) Terence Rattigan (d) Shelagh Delaney

458. Who is the author of the following plays: *A Sleep of Prisoners, A Phoenix Too Frequent, The Lady's Not for Burning,* and *Venus Observed* ?
(a) Christopher Fry (b) Christopher Isherwood (c) W.H. Auden (d) Robert Bolt

459. *Westward Ho*! was written by
(a) Charles Kingsley (b) John Buchan (c) George Chapman (d) Ben Jonson

460. Who said, 'A drama critic is a person who surprises the playwright by informing him of what he meant'?
(a) George Bernard Shaw (b) Robert Bolt (c) Wilson Mizner (d) Arnold Wesker

461. Which is the world's shortest dramatic work?
(a) *Not I* (b) *Breath* (c) *Footfalls* (d) *Radio I*

462. Beaumarchais' comedy *The Barber of Saville* (1775) was made into an opera by
(a) Mozart (b) Bizet (c) Rossini (d) Gounod

463. Pierre Augustine Beaumarchais wrote the brilliant comedy *The Marriage of Figaro* (1784), which was made into an opera, by
(a) Rossini (b) Gounod (c) Mozart (d) Verdi

464. This dramatist came into prominence with his play *Rosencrantz and Guildenstern Are Dead* (1966). Who is he?
(a) John Osborne (b) Arnold Wesker (c) Tom Stoppard (d) Trevor Griffiths

465. Of the following plays which are Corneille's and which are Racine's?
(a) *Phèdre* (b) *Athalie* (c) *Le Cid* (d) *Cinna*

466. Which among the following of Jean Cocteau's works was not filmed?
(a) *The Infernal Machine* (b) *Orphée* (c) *The Blood of a Poet* (d) *Beauty and the Beast*

467. This play when first performed at the Abbey Theatre, Dublin, so shocked the audience that there was a riot. Which is it?
(a) *Cathleen ni Houlihan* by Yeats (b) *Spreading the News* by Lady Gregory (c) *The Playboy of the Western World* by Synge (d) *The Shewing-up of Blanco Posnet* by Shaw

468. Oscar Wilde's *Salome* was illustrated by a contemporary illustrator. Who?
(a) William Morris (b) J.M. Whistler (c) Aubrey Beardsley (d) Lord Alfred Douglas

169. In which language did Ibsen originally write?
(a) Norwegian (b) Swedish (c) Finnish (d) German
(Russian is not given as a choice, although at an

interview a person who had written a paper on Ibsen's influence on... offered Russian in answer to this question)

470. Among the plays which ushered in French Surrealistic Theatre was one by Jean Cocteau, whose set was designed by Picasso. Which play was it?
(a) *The Breasts of Tiresias* (b) *Ubu* (c) *Parade* (d) *The Wedding on the Eiffel Tower*

471. Who wrote *Peter Pan?*
(a) A.A. Milne (b) Ken Barrington (c) Enid Blyton (d) Sir James Barry

472. 'Dear Sir,

I would be obliged if you would kindly explain to me the meaning of your play "The Birthday Party". These are the points I do not understand:

    1. Who are the two men ?
    2. Where did Stanley come from?
    3. Were they all supposed to be normal?

You will appreciate that without the answers to my questions, I cannot fully understand your play.

Yours faithfully,
Mrs ———'

The dramatist answered:
'Dear Madam,

I would be obliged if you would kindly explain to me the meaning of your letter. These are the points which I do not understand:

    1. Who are you ?

2. Where do you come from?

3. Are you supposed to be normal?

You will appreciate that without the answers to my questions, I cannot fully understand your letter.

Yours faithfully,'

Who is the dramatist?

(a) John Osborne (b) Arnold Wesker (c) Harold Pinter (d) Tom Stoppard

473. 'The Rising of the Moon' is one of the most well-known one-act plays to come out of Ireland. Who wrote it?
(a) J.M. Synge (b) Lady Gregory (c) W.B. Yeats (d) Edward Martyn

474. *A Game at Chess*, a comic drama, was written by
(a) T.S. Eliot (b) Thomas Middleton (c) James Agee (d) John Webster

475. Arthur Miller, the American playwright, who was hauled up before an enquiry committee started by Senator Joseph McCarthy, wrote a play condemning the witch hunt for Communists. Which play is it?
(a) *After the Fall* (b) *The Crucible* (e) *The Misfits* (d) *The Price*

476. Imamu Amiri Baraka, Black American author of *Dutchman* and *The Slave : two plays*, is better known by another name. Which is it?
(a) Charles Fuller (b) Langston Hughes (c) Robert Earl Hayden (d) Le Roi Jones

477. Which of the following plays by Eugene O' Neill is autobiographical ?
(a) *Beyond the Horizon* (b) *Ah, Wilderness!* (c) *A Moon for the Misbegotten* (d) *Long Day's Journey into Night*

478. Estragon and Vladimir, Lucky and Pozzo, which play do they appear in ?
(a) *Roots* (b) *Look Back in Anger* (c) *Waiting for Godot* (d) *A Taste of Honey*

479. Of the following plays by Arthur Miller which one did he write earliest ?
(a) *All My Sons* (b) *Death of a Salesman* (c) *A View from the Bridge* (d) *Crucibles*

480. Of the names of the following plays of Strindberg which one contains a mistake ?
(a) *Miss Julie* (b) *A Dream Play* (c) *A Ghostly Sonata* (d) *The Dance of Death*

481. Covent Garden, London's opera and produce market (until recently) district features prominently in one of the following plays. Which?
(a) *Chicken Soup with Barley* (b) *The Kitchen* (c) *Pygmalion* (d) *A Taste of Honey*

482. Arthur Miller wrote a screenplay especially for his wife, Marilyn Monroe. Which is it ?
(a) *The Misfits* (b) *A View from the Bridge* (c) *After the Fall* (d) *Death of a Salesman*

483. Of the following plays, one is not by Brecht. Which?
(a) *Man Is Man* (b) *The Measures Taken* (c) *He Who Said Yes/He Who Said No* (d) *The Dance of Death*

484. Of the following, all Samuel Beckett's, which originally appeared in French?
(a) *Molloy* (b) *Malone Dies* (c) *Waiting for Godot* (d) *Murphy*

485. Bertolt Brecht is chiefly known as a dramatist, but he also wrote a novel. Which is it?
(a) *Kafka's Other Trial* (b) *Threepenny Novel* (c) *The Thirty Years War* (d) *Three Hostages*

486. Athol Fugord (b. 1932) is an important South African dramatist who has written feelingly about blacks, coloureds and poor whites. Identify his play from the list.
(a) *Kongi's Harvest* (b) *The Lion and the Jewel* (c) *Death and the King's Horseman* (d) *Boesman and Lena*

487. Harold Pinter (b.1930), an eminent dramatist, author of *The Birthday Party, The Caretaker, The Homecoming,* etc., has also written screenplays. Which of the following is his?
(a) *Tess of the D'Urbervilles* (b) *Schindler's List* (c) *The French Lieutenant's Woman* (d) *The Quiet American*

488. *A Man for All Seasons,* a play on the life of Sir Thomas More, is his best known work. Who is he?
(a) John Arden (b) Arnold Wesker (c) John Osborne

(d) Robert Bolt

489. *Chicken Soup with Barley, Roots, I'm Talking about Jerusalem,* and *Kitchen* were all written by a 'Kitchen Sink dramatist.' Who is he?
(a) Shelagh Delaney (b) Arnold Wesker (c) Terence Rattigan (d) Noel Coward

8

POETRY PARADE

490. I.A. Richards, one of the most influential critics of this century, was a Fellow at Cambridge, where as an exercise of practical criticism he handed out to students unsigned poems for their review. The results were often interesting. Which of the following poets were condemned by the students and which did they like?
(a) G.A. Studdert Kennedy (b) Gerard Manley Hopkins (c) D.H. Lawrence (d) J.D.C. Pellew

491. 'In Reflections on Ice-breaking' a poet observed:
    Candy
    Is dandy
    But liquor
    Is quicker.
Who?
(a) Don Marquis (b) Oscar Wilde (c) Ogden Nash
(d) E.E. Cummings

492. Francis Thompson wrote poems about
    (a)   Nature (b) Sex (c) War (d) God

493.   'When lovely woman stoops to folly
         And finds too late that men betray,
         What charm can soothe her melancholy,
         What art can wash her guilt away?'
This a stanza of Godsmith's in *The Vicar of Wakefield*
simply cries to be parodied, and so it was. Where?
(a) 'The Love Song of J. Alfred Prufrock'
(b) 'Portrait of a Lady' (c) *The Waste Land* (d) 'Ash-
Wednesday'

494. 'Rose Aylmer, whom these wakeful eyes
     May weep, but never see,
     A night of memories and sighs
     I consecrate to thee.'
—   The lines are addressed to a young woman
who lies buried in a Calcutta cemetery. Who is the
poet?
(a) Charles Lamb (b) William Cory (c) Rudyard
Kipling (d) Walter Savage Landor

495. 'Next to, of course God, America, I
     Love you, land of pilgrims and so forth, Oh!'
The original punctuation is modified, but who
wrote these lines?
(a) Walt Whitman (b) Allen Ginsburg
(c) E.E. Cummings (d) Robert Lowell

496. Who wrote:
         'The rain it raineth on the just
         And also on the unjust fella:
         But chiefly on the just, because

The unjust steals the just's umbrella.'
(a)   Bertolt Brecht (b) Nicholas Breton (c) Lord
Bowen (d) Elizabeth Bowen

497.   'Against the bridal day, which was not long:
          Sweet Thames! run softly, till I end my song.'
          These lines are from
(a)   Spenser's 'Prothalamion' (b) Eliot's   Waste
Land (c) Marlowe's Hero and Leander (d) Spenser's
'Epithalamion'

498. 'Change in a trice!
     The lillies and languors of virtue
     For the raptures and roses of vice.'
     Where do these lines occur?
(a)   Swinburne , Dolores (b) Ernest Dowson, 'Non
Sum Qualis Eram'   (c) Oscar Wilde, Salome
(d) D.H. Lawrence, Amores

499.   'Are changed, changed utterly:
          A terrible beauty is born.'
—   Thus ends a famous poem of the present
century. Can you name the poet?
(a)   William Morris (b) W.B. Yeats (c) Edward
Thomas (d) Dylan Thomas

500.   'Bald heads forgetful of their sins,
          Old, learned, respectable bald heads
          Edit and annotate the lines
          That young men, tossing on their beds,
          Rhymed out in love's despair

To flatter beauty's ignorant ear.'
Who wrote this indictment of scholars?
(a) Jonathan Swift (b) William Wordsworth
(c) W.B. Yeats (d) W.H. Auden

501. Who wrote
'I'm tired of love: I'm still more tired of rhyme
But money gives me pleasure all the time'?
(a) Lord Byron (b) Oscar Wilde (c) Robert Graves
(d) Hillaire Belloc

502. 'The expense of spirit in a waste of shame
Is lust in action…'
Whose lines are these?
(a) Cecil Day Lewis (b) Robert Graves (c) John
Donne (d) Shakespeare

503. 'All things counter, original, spare, strange;
Whatever is fickle, freckled (who knows
how?)
With swift, slow; sweet, sour; adazzle, dim;
He fathers-forth whose beauty is past change:
Praise him.'
— Whose exhortation is this?
(a) Robert Browning(b) Gerard Manley Hopkins
(c) Alice Meynell (d) John Donne

504. 'The graves's a fine and private place,
But none, I think, do there embrace'
Whose lines are these?
(a) Fulke Greville (b) Henry King (c) Andrew

Marvell (d) John Donne

505. Who wrote, 'Oh to be in England,
Now that April's there'?
(a) Rupert Brooke (b) Peter Sellers (c) Robert
Browning (d) Anthony Burgess

506. Who wrote, 'Stone walls do not a prison make
Nor iron bars a cage...'?
(a) George Herbert (b) Robert Herrick (c) Richard
Lovelace (d) Ben Jonson

507. 'As civilization advances, poetry almost
necessarily declines.' Who said this about epic
poetry?
(a) Dr. Johnson (b) Matthew Arnold (c) Coleridge
(d) Macaulay

508.   'Sumer is icumen in
Lhude sing cuccu! — begins the thirteenth
century song. Who wrote, in parody,
'Winter is icumen in
Lhude sing goddam'?
(a) Henry Miller (b) D.H. Lawrence (c) Dylan
Thomas (d) Ezra Pound

509. 'The words of the dead man are modified in the
guts of the living', said
(a) W.B. Yeats (b) W.H. Auden (c) Stephen
Spender (d) T.S. Eliot

510. Who wrote the famous poem 'Adlestrop'?
(a) Edward Thomas (b) Dylan Thomas
(c) Thomas Hardy (d) T.S. Eliot

511. Who is the poet's guide in the *Divine Comedy* from the first circle of hell to its very depths, Judecca?
(a) Tasso (b) Epicurus (c) Vergil (d) Ovid

512. Which set of dates applies to Dante Alighieri?
(a) 1089-1156 (b) 1140-1230 (c) 1265-1321 (d) 1240-1299

513. In which century did Omar Khayyam write his Rubaiyat?
(a) Tenth (b) Eleventh (c) Sixteenth
(d) Seventeenth

514. This is a Cambridge poet writing on Cambridge:
'For Cambridge people rarely smile,
Being urban, squat, and packed with guile.'
Who is he?
(a) A.E. Housman (b) Rupert Brooke (c) Ted Hughes (d) Thom Gunn

515. Who said
'Let us honour if we can
The vertical man
Though we value none
But the horizontal one'?
(a) W.H. Auden (b) Kingsley Amis (c) Philip Larkin (d) Ted Hughes

516. Who said, 'a pretty girl who naked is/is worth half a million statues'?
(a) Eric Gill (b) Pablo Picasso (c) E.E. Cummings (d) Oscar Wilde

517. 'Over this damp grave I speak the words of my love:
I, with no rights in this matter,
Neither father nor lover.'
— Who wrote this on the death of his student, thrown by a horse?
(a) Theodore Roethke (b) Robert Graves (c) Cecil Day Lewis (d) John Betjeman

518. 'The best lack all conviction, while the worst Are full of passionate intensity.'
Where are these lines to be found?
(a) Pope, *Dunciad* (b) Byron, *Don Juan* (c) Tennyson, *In Memoriam* (d) Yeats, 'The Second Coming'

519. A satirist said,
'Ask you what provocation I have had?
The strong antipathy of good to bad.'
Who?
(a) John Dryden (b) Alexander Pope (c) Jonathan Swift (d) Lord Byron

520. 'This is my play's last scene, here heavens appoint My pilgrimage's last mile'.
To which of the following do these lines belong?

(a) Jean Anouilh : *Becket* (b) John Donne : ' Holy Sonnets ' (c) T.S.Eliot : *Murder in the Cathedral* (d) Gerard Manley Hopkins : Sonnet

521. 'No Spring,nor summer beauty hath such grace,
As I have seen in one autumnal face.'
Who wrote these lines?
(a) William Wordsworth (b) William Shakespeare
(c) John Milton (d) John Donne

522. 'The houses are all gone under the sea.
The dancers are all gone under the hill'
Who wrote these lines ?
(a) T.S.Eliot (b) W.B.Yeats (c) John Betjeman
(d) W.H.Auden

523. 'Strange to me, sounds the wind that blows
By the masthead, in the lonely night
Maybe 'tis the sea whistling — feigning joy
To hide its fright
Like a village boy
That trembling past the churchyard goes.'
Who wrote this imagist poem ?
(a) T.E.Hulme (b) Hilda Doolittle (c) F.S.Flint
(d) Ezra Pound

524. Match the Bard with the name
1. The Bard of Rydal Mount a. Robert Burns
2. The Bard of Ayrshire b. Alexander Pope
3. The Bard of Twickenham c. Shakespeare
4. The Bard of Avon d. Wordsworth

525. A Poet Laureate made the modest claim, 'I don't think that since Shakespeare there has been such a master of the English language as I.' Who is he ?
(a) Wordsworth (b) Tennyson (c) C.Day Lewis (d) John Betjeman

526. 'If the doors of perception were cleansed everything would appear to man as it is, infinite.' Who wrote this ?
(a) William Wordsworth (b) Aldous Huxley (c) John Keats (d) William Blake

527. *Les Fleurs du mal* or *The Flowers of Evil* (1857) is the work of
(a) Rimbaud (b) Villon (c) Baudelaire (d) Verlaine

528. What are the Christian names of W.H.Auden ?
(a) William Henry (b) Walter Hyram (c) Wystan Hugh (d) Winston Horace

529. Charles Hamilton Sorley, Isaac Rosenberg, Wilfred Owen, and Rupert Brooke were all First World War poets. What else have they in common ?
(a) All were published posthumously (b) All came from Oxford (c) All were killed in action (d) *The New Oxford Book of English Verse* ignores them all.

530. Who among the following poets of the Auden generation ended up as a Poet Laureate ?
(a) W.H.Auden (b) Stephen Spender (c) Louis MacNeice (d) Cecil Day Lewis

531. Of the following twentieth-century poets only one is not a Poet Laureate. Who is the exception ?
(a) John Masefield (b) Robert Bridges (c) Robert Graves (d) Cecil Day Lewis

532. Who was the first ever Poet Laureate ?
(a) Ben Jonson (b) Alexander Pope (c) John Dryden (d) William Wordsworth

533. *Blackwood Magazine* carried out a long series of attacks,from 1817, against what it called the 'Cockney School of Poetry.' Who among the following were the targets of their attack ?
(a) Leigh Hunt (b) William Wordsworth (c) William Hazlitt (d) John Keats

534. Educated at Oxford and Principal of Poona College (1856-61), he is remembered in India for *The Light of Asia* or *The Great Renunciation*(1879) - a very long poem about the Buddha. Who is he ?
(a) Sir William Jones (b) Sir Edwin Arnold (c) J.W. McCrinde (d) A.B. Keith

535. As many as twelve Pulitzer Prizes are awarded each year for journalism. However, these prizes are also given for poetry and other creative writing. One American poet won the prize in 1924, 1931, 1937, and 1943. Who is he?
(a) Wallace Stevens (b) Marianne Moore (c) Robert Lowell (d) Robert Frost

536. *The Golden Treasury* is perhaps the most famous anthology of English poetry still current today. Who is the compiler?

(a) Laurence Binyon (b) Cecil Day Lewis (c) F.T. Palgrave (d) Helen Gardner

537. 'I am monarch [not *the monarch*] of all I survey' is a well-known poem on Alexander Selkirk who lived for five years in an uninhabited island. Who wrote the poem?

(a) Thomas Gray (b) Oliver Goldsmith (c) William Cowper (d) Daniel Defoe

538. '... charm'd magic casements, opening on the foam/Of perilious seas...' Keats was thinking of a particular painting, viz., *The Enchanted Castle,* when he wrote this. Who is the painter?

(a) Thomas Gainsborough (b) Claude Lorrain (c) John Constable (d) J.M.W. Turner

539. 'Not charioted by Bacchus and his pards...' wrote Keats in 'Ode to a Nightingale'. He had a particular painting in his mind. Whose?

(a) Gainsborough (b) Rembrandt (c) Titian (d) Bruegel

540. W.H. Auden wrote his poem 'Musee des Beaux Arts' ('About suffering they were never wrong/ The Old Masters....) on *The Fall of Icarus.* Who painted it?

(a) Eugene Delacroix (b) William Hogarth

(c) Pieter Bruegel (d) Rembrandt

541. Who invented clerihews, four-line poems rhyming aa bb? Example:

> Sir Christopher Wren
> Said 'I'm going to dine with some men.
> If anybody calls
> Say I'm designing St. Paul's'.

(a) Edward Lear (b) Edmund Clerihew (c) E.C. Bentley (d) Hillaire Belloc

542.
> 'Jenny kissed me when we met
> Jumping from the chair she sat in;
> Time, you thief, who love to get
> Sweets into your list, put that in.'

— Who wrote this? Jenny, incidentally, was Mrs. Carlyle.

(a) Byron (b) Leigh Hunt (c) W.S. Landor (d) Thomas Hood

543. Who sounded the warning

> 'You should not take a fellow eight years old
> And make him swear to never kiss the girls.'

(a) Robert Graves (b) William Blake (c) Dylan Thomas (d) Robert Browning

544. Who wrote, 'How beastly the bourgeois is especially the male of the species'?
(a) D.H. Lawrence (b) Karl Marx (c) Vladimir Mayakovsky (d) Stephen Spender

545. 'It's no go, my honey love, it's no go, my poppet;
Work your hands from day to day, the winds will
blow the profit.'
— Whose lines are these ?
(a) Louis MacNeice (b) W.H. Auden (c) Stephen
Spender (d) Cecil Day Lewis

546. 'A politician is an arse upon which everyone has sat
except a man'. A poet's definition. Which poet?
(a) Walt Whitman (b) Carl Sandburg
(c) E.E. Cummings (d) Hart Crane

547. Who declared so defiantly:
'I'll publish, right or wrong:
Fools are my theme, let satire be my song.'
(a) Jonathan Swift (b) Alexander Pope (c) Lord
Byron (d) Oscar Wilde

548. Who said 'Poetry is more philosophical and of
higher value than history'?
(a) Lord Acton (b) Benjamin Jowett (c) Aristotle
(d) W.B. Yeats

549. Who said, 'Poetry makes nothing happen'?
(a) Plato (b) Coleridge (c) W.H. Auden
(d) Matthew Arnold

550. 'The clever man who cries
The catch-cries of the clown,
The beating down of the wise
And great Art beaten down.'
— Who is the poet?

(a) W.B. Yeats (b) T.S. Eliot (c) Dylan Thomas
(d) R.S. Thomas

551. Who said
> 'I'm afraid there's many a spectacled sod
> Prefers the British Museum to God.'

(a) George Gordon Lord Byron (b) A.C.
Swinburne (c) W.H. Auden (d) Hillaire Belloc

552. 'What men call gallantry, and gods adultery,
> Is much more common where the climate's
> sultry'.

In which of the following poems does Byron say
this?
(a) *Don Juan* (b) *Childe Harold's Pilgrimage*
(c) *Destruction of Sennacherib* (d) *Beppo*

553. 'The man recover'd of the bite,
> The dog it was that died.'

— Whose poem ends with these lines?
(A) Alexander Pope (b) Oliver Goldsmith
(b) Jonathan Swift (d) Dr. Johnson

554. Who wrote, 'Lilies that fester smell far worse than
weeds'?
(a) Shakespeare (b) Ben Jonson (c) Webster
(d) Ford

555. 'If the red slayer thinks he slays,
> Or if the slain think he is slain,

They know not well the subtle ways
I keep, and pass, and turn again.'
Where are these lines to be found?
(a) In the *Bhagavadgeeta* (b) In the Briha-
daranyaka Upanishad (c) In T.S. Eliot's *Four
Quartets* (d) In R.W. Emerson's 'Brahma'

556. 'The Moving Finger writes; and having writ,
Moves on: nor all thy Piety nor Wit
Shall lure it back to cancel half a Line,
Nor all thy Tears wash out a Word of it.'
— Who said this?
(a) Shakespeare (b) William Blake (c) P.B. Shelley
(d) Edward Fitzgerald

557. 'And there I shut her wild wild eyes
With kisses four.'
— Name the poem in which these lines occur.
(a) *Hyperion* (b) *Endymion* (c) *Lamia* (d) *'La Belle
Dame Sans Merci'*

558. 'I strove with none; for none was worth my
                                                strife;
Nature I loved, and, next to nature, Art;
I warmed both hands before the fire of life;
It sinks, and I am ready to depart.'
This is the complete poem. Who wrote it?
(a) Charles Lamb (b) William Savage Landor
(c) Thomas Hood (d) Leigh Hunt

559. 'Go lovely rose

Tell her that wastes her time and me,
That now she knows
When I resemble her to thee,
How sweet and fair she seems to be.'
Who wrote these lines?
(a) Robert Herrick (b) Ben Jonson (c) Edmund Waller (d) Richard Crashaw

560. In a celebrated preface this author wrote, 'Above all, this book is not concerned with poetry. The subject of it is War, and the pity of the War.' Who is he?
(a) Julian Grenfell (b) Sigfried Sassoon (c) Maurice Cornford (d) Wilfred Owen

561. Where do the following occur?
        'Winter is come and gone,
        But grief returns with the revolving year.'
(a) Shelley, 'Adonais' (b) Tennyson, *In Memoriam* (c) Rossetti, 'The Blessed Damozel' (d) Arnold, 'Requiescat'

562. 'Blossom by blossom the spring begins'. In which poem does this line occur?
(a) William Blake, 'Spring' (b) Thomas Nash, 'Spring' (c) Swinburne, 'When the hounds of spring' (d) Tennyson, 'Early Spring'

563. 'The rose was awake all night for your sake,
        Knowing your promise to me;
        The lilies and roses were all aware,

They sighed for the dawn and thee.'
These lines are from:
(a) Tennyson: *Maud* (b) Swinburne: 'Hymn to Proserpine' (c) Shelley: Sonnet (d) Meredith: *Modern Love*

564. Who is the author of this poem on cancer of which he died?

> 'My final word, before I'm done,
> Is "Cancer can be great fun."
> Thanks to the nurses and Nye Bevan
> The NHS is quite like a heaven
> Provided one confronts the tumour
> With a sufficient sense of humour.'

(a) W.H. Auden (b) Sylvia Plath (c) J.B.S. Haldane (d) James Cameron

565.
> 'To keep your marriage brimming
> With love in the marriage cup,
> Whenever you're wrong, admit it;
> Whenever you're right, shut up.'

Sound advice from a poet who studied women carefully. Who is he?
(a) W.S. Gilbert (b) Robert Frost (c) Ogden Nash (d) Spike Milligan

566.
> 'One more Unfortunate/Weary of breath/
> Rashly importunate,/Gone to her death!'—

Thus begins 'The Bridge of Sighs'. Who wrote it?
(a) Walter Scott (b) Charles Lamb (c) Thomas Hood (d) Robert Southey

567.   'Grishkin in nice: her Russian eye
         Is underlined for emphasis;
         Uncorseted, her friendly bust
         Gives promise of pneumatic bliss.'
Whose lines are these and from where?
(a) W.H. Auden (b) Philip Larkin (c) T.S. Eliot
(d) C. Day Lewis

568. 'A heavy weight of hours has chained and bowed
One too like thee: tameless, and swift, and proud.'
Whose lines are these?
(a)   Byron (b) Shelley (c) Keats (d) Wordsworth

569. In 'Solitary Reaper' Wordsworth puts the reaper's
song above the cuckoo's 'breaking the silence of the
seas/Among the farthest Hebrides'. Where are the
Hebrides?
(a)   Off the Scottish Coast (b) Off the Irish Coast
(c) On the Caribbean Sea (d) Off the Newfoundland
Coast

570.   'We look before and after,
         And pine for what is not:
         Our sincerest laughter
         With some pain is fraught;
         Our sweetest songs are those that tell of
                        saddest thoughts'
— The author is
(a) Wordsworth (b) Byron (c) Shelley (d) Keats

571. Sceptre and crown

Must tumble down,
And in the dust be equal made
With the poor crooked scythe and spade.'
Who wrote these lines?
(a)Herrick (b) Ben Jonson (c) Shirley (d) Marvell

572. A poet wrote this epitaph for himself:
'Here he lies where he longed to be;
Home is the sailor, home from the sea,
And the hunter home from hill'.
Who ?
(a) Walter de la Mare (b) Tennyson (c) Robert Bridges (d) R.L.Stevenson

573.　　'Willows whiten, aspens quiver,
Little breezes dusk and shiver
Thro' the wave that runs for ever
By the island in the river.'
From which poem is this stanza taken?
(a)　Scott, *The Lady of the Lake* (b)Tennyson, *'The Lady of Shalott'* (c) Swinburne, *Atalanta in Calydon* (d) Keats, *Endymion*

574.　　'He played an ancient ditty, long since mute,
In provence called "La belle dame sans
merci".'
—　In which poem do these lines occur?
(a)　'La Belle Dame Sans Merci' (b) 'Porphyro and Madeline' (c) 'Adonis' (d) 'The Eve of St. Agnes'

575.'Oh East is East, and West is West and never the

twain shall meet.' In which poem of Kipling does this line occur?

(a) The Ballad of East and West (b) Gunga Din (c) If (d) The White Man's Burden

576. To which century do Heinrich Heine's romantic lyrics belong?

(a) Late eighteenth century (b) Early nineteenth century (c) Middle of the nineteenth century (d) Late nineteenth century

577. Of the following, one is *not* a silver poet of 16th century. Who?

(a) Thomas Wyatt (b) Philip Sidney (c) Edmund Spenser (d) Walter Raleigh

578. Which was the first English poetry anthology?

(a) *England's Parnassus*   (b) *England's Helicon* (c) *Tottell's Miscellany*   (d) Palgraves's *Golden Treasury*

579. 'The Fleshly School of Poetry' comprised some of the following. Name who.

(a) Dante Gabriel Rossetti (b) A.C. Swinburne (c) Robert Browning (d) William Morris

580. Three well-known treatments of the Troilus-Cressida story exist in English. Of the following which one is inauthentic?

(a) *Troilus and Criseyde* (b) *The Trials of Cresseid* (c) *The Testament of Cresseid* (d) *Troilus and Cressida*

581. Of the following, who is not a Scottish Chaucerian?
(a) Gower (b) Dunbar (c) Henryson (d) Gavin Douglas

582. Which poets did Southey include in the Satanic School?
(a) Thomas Moore (b) P.B. Shelley (c) Lord Byron (d) John Keats

583. One of the following is not regarded as a Georgian poet. Who?
(a) Gerard Manley Hopkins (b) W.H. Davies (c) John Masefield (d) Walter de la Mare

584. Who has been called the most venomous and malicious of the great English poets?
(a) Alexander Pope (b) Jonathan Swift (c) Samuel Johnson (d) Dylan Thomas

585. Which contemporary of Pope was satirized by him as Atticus?
(a) Jonathan Swift (b) Joseph Addison (c) Richard Steele (d) Lord Harvey

586. Of the following, which is not Chaucer's work?
(a) *The Paliament of Fowls* (b) *Book of the Duchess* (c) *Legend of Good Women* (d) *The Testament of Cresseid*

587. The Pre-Raphaelite Brotherhood, which formally first met in 1848, comprised poets, critics, and

painters. Among the poets its most notable follower was
(a) George Meredith (b) Christina Rossetti (c) Dante Gabriel Rossetti (d) A.C. Swinburne

588. But for the poet Robet Bridges, who edited a posthumous collection, this major English poet might have remained unknown. Who is he ?
(a) W.H. Davies (b) Walter de la Mare (c) Gerard Manley Hopkins (d) Ernest Dowson

589. Who among the following are writers of the beat generation?
(a) Allen Ginsberg (b) William Burroughs (c) Lawrence Ferlinghetti (d) Jack Kerouac

590. 'Namby-Pamby's doubly mild,
Once a man and twice a child. . .
Now he pumps his little wits
All by little tiny bits.'
— Who is this original Namby -Pamby ?
(a) George Southey (b) John Suckling (c) Ambrose Philips (d) Colley Cibber

591. One of the following poets qualifies for the title 'England's Fattest Major Poet'. Guess who.
(a) S.T. Coleridge (b) John Dryden (c) Robert Southey (d) W. H. Auden

592. Stephen Spender, W.H. Auden, Louis MacNeice, and Christopher Isherwood shared one thing in

common. Which?

(a) They were class-fellows at Eton (b) They all went to the Spanish Civil War (c) They were contemporaries at Oxford (d) They all became U.S. citizens

593. The most celebrated poet of the dramatic monologue was Robert Browning. Who, among the following, have also used this form successfully ?

(a) Thomas Hardy (b) W.B. Yeats (c) Robert Frost (d) Ted Hughes

594. 'I confess freely to you, I could never look upon a monkey, without very mortifying reflections'. Who wrote this ?

(a) Alexander Pope (b) Charles Darwin (c) William Congreve (d) Jonathan Swift

595.   ' I wish I loved the Human Race;
         I wish I loved its silly face;
         I wish I liked the way it walks;
         I wish I liked the way it talks;
         And when I'm introduced to one
         I wish I thought *What Jolly Fun!*'

Who wrote that?

(a) Jonathan Swift (b) Walter Raleigh (c) Lord Byron (d) W.H. Auden

596. In whose poem does this refrain occur?

         'I have been faithful to thee, Cynara!

in my fashion'.
(a) A.C. Swinburne (b) Ernest Dowson (c) Edward
Thomas (d) Dylan Thomas

597. Who introduced the Petrarchan sonnet form
(octave and sestet) into English ?
(a) Geoffrey Chaucer (b) William Shakespeare
(c) Edmund Spenser (d) Wyatt and Surrey

598. Caligrammes, a term coined in this century, refer to
poems written in particular shapes reflecting their
subject matter, e.g., butterflies, pillars, wings, etc.
Who is the first English poet to have used this
form ?
(a) Edmund Spenser (b) John Donne (c) George
Herbert (d) Richard Crashaw

599. Which English poet most frequently uses the
ancient poetical name of Albion (from Latin *albus,*
white, probably referring to the white cliffs of
Dover) for England in his poetry?
(a)   John Keats (b) P.B. Shelley (c) William Blake
(d) Elizabeth Barrett Browning

600. The literature of the Beat Generation in the US has
some of the following characteristics. Which?
(a) Intense sexual passion (b) Disengagement
(c) 'Street' language (d) Spontaneity

601. Ariel, some kind of spirit, has been quite popular
among poets and dramatists. In the *Tempest* he is

a liberated spirit, in *Paradise Lost* he is one of the rebel angels, in *The Rape of the Lock* he looks after women, and in Andre Maurois's biography, he is Shelley. Which twentieth century poet used his name as the title of a group of poems?
(a) Philp Larkin (b) Sylvia Plath (c) Ted Hughes (d) T.S. Eliot

602. Who, among the following, are regarded as Scottish Chaucerians?
(a) William Dunbar (b) Robert Henryson (c) John Lydgate (d) Gavin Douglas

603. The first edition of Palgraves *Golden Treasury* omitted the work of some major poets. Whose, among the following?
(a) Andrew Marvell (b) Christina Rossetti (c) William Blake (d) Robert Burns

604. The number of pilgrims going to Canterbury together, in Chaucer's *Canterbury Tales*, has been variously computed. How many does Chaucer say there were?
(a) 22 (b) 27 (c) 29 (d) 31

605. Who is Thyrsis in the poem of the same name written by Matthew Arnold?
(a) Percy Bysshe Shelley (b) John Keats (c) Arthur Hallam (d) Arthur Hugh Clough

606. A ship is driven towards the South Pole by a storm,

a bird appears . . . and then things begin to happen. In whose work do you find this situation?
(a) Walter de la Mare (b) S.T. Coleridge (c) Joseph Conrad (d) C.S. Forester

607. Which is the correct spelling of the name of the poem ?
(a) The Lady of Shallott (b) The Lady of Shalot
(c) The Lady of Shalott (d) The Lady of Shallot

608. 'To see a World in a grain of rand,
   And a Heaven in a wild flower,
   Hold Infinity in the palm of your hand,
   And Eternity in an hour.'
   — Who wrote this?
(a) Alice Meynell (b) William Blake (c) Evelyn Underhill (d) Fancis Thompson

609. 'Others abide our question. Thou art free.' Matthew Arnold wrote this in a famous sonnet. Who is it addressed to ?
(a) Socrates (b) Plato (c) Homer (d) Shakespeare

610. Haiku, a short lyric of seventeen syllables in all, 5+7+5, has its country of origin in
(a) China (b) Japan (c) India (d) Iceland

611. Which among the following works of Milton is a poetic drama ?
(a) *Areopagitica* (b) *Comus* (c) *Paradise Regained*
(d) *Samson Agonistes*

612. Which English poet referred to Oxford as 'that sweet city with her dreaming spires'?
(a) Robert Graves (b) Matthew Arnold (c) W.H. Auden (d) Alexander Pope

613. 'Say not the struggle not availeth' is an optimistic sonnet written by a poet who also wrote the very cynical 'The Latest Decalogue'. Who is the poet?
(a) Samuel Johnson (b) Jonathan Swift (c) Thomas Lovell Beddoes (d) Arthur Hugh Clough

614. *The Vicar of Wakefield* , an important novel in the history of English fiction, was written by Oliver Goldsmith, who was also a poet. Can you name his most well-known poem?
(a) *The Task* (b) *John Gilpin* (c) *The Progress of Poesy* (d) *The Deserted Village*

615.   'He gave the little wealth he had
        To build a house for fools and mad:
        And showed by one satiric touch,
        No nation wanted it so much.'
To which satirist do these lines refer?
(a) Jonathan Swift (b) Alexander Pope (c) Dr. Johnson (d) The Earl of Rochester

616. Which of the following birds did Wordsworth write poems on?
(a) Skylark (b) Green Linnet (c) Eagle (d) Parrot

617. How many Chapters or *Suras* does the Koran

have?
(a) 96 (b) 100 (c) 114 (d) 137

618. Authors as diverse as Swinburne, Yeats, Borges and Baudelaire have admired his poetry and fiction; some of them have been influenced. Who is this author of the macabre and the pathological who wrote a poem called 'The Raven'?
(a) Ralph Waldo Emerson (b) John Greenleaf Whittier (c) Edgar Allan Poe (d) Herman Melville

619. An American poet professed his love for American place names, some of which are: Lost Mule Flat, Little French Lick, Salem, Bleeding-Heart-Yard, Painted Post, and Skunktown Plain. It was he who wrote the memborable line: 'Bury my heart at Wounded Knee'. Who is he?
(a) Henry Wadsworth Longfellow (b) Walt Whitman (c) Edwin Arlington Robinson (d) Stephen Vincent Benet

620. An American poet, first published by Emerson, had the Indian misfortune of being accepted in his own country only after foreign recognition, in this case England's. He wrote the great elegy on Lincoln, 'When Lilacs Last in the Dooryard Bloomed'. Who is the poet?
(a) Walt Whitman (b) Henry David Thoreau (c) John Greenleaf Whittier (d) James Russell Lowell

621. After a night's heavy bombardment by the British a poet saw the American flag still fluttering on Fort Mc Henry, and was inspired to compose 'The Star-Spangled Banner' which by an Act of Congress became the American national anthem. Who wrote it?
(a) Philip Freneau (b) Joseph Hopkinson (c) Francis Scott Key (d) John Pierpont

622. Two sisters collaborated in writing 'Twinkle, twinkle little star'. Which pair?
(a) Ann and Emily Bronte (b) Emily and Elizabeth Dickinson (c) Ann and Jane Taylor (d) Christina and Georgina Rossetti

623. Who wrote the Bab Ballads?
(a) W.S. Gilbert (b) A. Sullivan(c) Gilbert and Sullivan (d) Parry and Stanford

624. Who wrote 'The Charge of the Light Brigade'?
(a)Browning (b) Tennyson (c)Wilfred Owen (d) Rupert Brooke

625. 'The Scholar-Gipsy' is perhaps the most famous poem written about Oxford. Who wrote it?
(a) Lewis Carroll (b) Andrew Marvell (c) Gerard Manley Hopkins (d) Matthew Arnold

626. One of the following poems is not by Robert Frost. Which?
(a) 'Birches' (b) 'The Road Not Taken' (c) 'Autumn

Landscape' (d) 'The Death of a Hired Man'

627. 'Casabianca' ('The boy stood on the burning deck')
was written by
(a) Anne Bronte (b) Emily Dickinson (c) Felicia
Hemans (d) Emily Post

628. He wrote the much-admired poem 'The Traveller'
but remains famous as the writer of a comedy in
which a maid at an inn is the heroine. Who is he and
what is the play?
(a) Richard Brinsley Sheridan (b) William Cowper
(c) Oliver Goldsmith (d) Thomas Gray

629. His City Lights bookshop in San Francisco was the
centre of Beat Generation poets. He was also a
prominent Beat poet. Who is he?
(a) Allen Ginsberg (b) Gregory Corso (c) Jack
Kerouac (d) Lawrence Ferlinghetti

630 This poet advocated 'the hard dry image' in poetry
and was one of the main influences on imagist
poetry. His poems, five in mumber, were
published in an anthology in 1912 as his 'Complete
Poetical Works'. Who is he?
(a) F.S. Flint (b) Ford Madox Hueffer (c) Richard
Aldington (d) T.E. Hulme

631. *Howl* (1956), a long poem which criticises a large
number of American values, is one of the most
important literary documents of the Beat

Generation. Who wrote it?
(a) Gregory Corso (b) Allen Ginsberg (c) Lawrence Ferlinghetti (d) Gary Snyder

632. He is the most important lyric poet of 20th century Germany and wrote *Sonnets to Orpheus*. Who is he ?
(a) Rainer Maria Rilke (b) Friedrich Holderlin (c) Heinrich Heine (d) Georg Heym

633. This person is known today not so much as a writer of critical articles and the weekly *Examiner,* which he edited, but as the author of Abou Ben Adhem" Who is he?
(a) William Hazlitt (b) Charles Lamb (c) Leigh Hunt (d) Coventry Patmore

634. The passing of youth and mortality are the themes of *A Shropshire Lad* — a book of poems distinguished by its haunting melancholy. Who wrote it?
(a) Thomas Hardy (b) Robert Bridges (c) A.E. Housman (d)Stevie smith

635. 'Mohini Chatterjee' is the name of a poem written in 1928. Who wrote it?
(a) Robert Bridges (b) W.B Yeats (c) Walter de la Mare (d) Sarojini Naidu

636. The following lines were written about the World War I dead. Who wrote them?

'They shall not grow old, as we that are left
                              grow old:
Age shall not weary them, nor the years
                              condemn,
At the going down of the sun and in the
                              morning
We will remember them.'
(a) Rupert Brooke (b) Laurence Binyon (c) Wilfred
Owen (d) Robert Graves

637.   *Alba*
As cool as the pale wet leaves of lily of valley
She lay beside me at dawn.
Who wrote this imagist poem?
(a) F.S. Flint (b) Ezra Pound (c) T.E Hulme (d) H.D.

9

FICTION : HIGH, MIDDLE, AND LOWBROW

638. In which novel does one of Anthony Burgess's characters say 'Bath twice a day to be really clean, once a day to be passably clean, once a week to avoid being a public menace'?
(a) *The Malayan Trilogy* (b) *Enderby Outside* (c) *Inside Mr. Enderby* (d) *Earthly Powers*

639. 'Alex and his three droogs tolchok an old vec, razrez his books, pull of his outer platties and take a malenky bit of cutter.' This is nadsat—the teenage argot of a not-too-distant future. Which book gives us a taste of it?
(a) *Finnegans Wake* by James Joyce (b) *More Pricks Than Kicks* by Samuel Beckett (c) *Blood and Guts in High School* by Kathy Acker (d) *A Clockwork Orange* by Anthony Burgess

640. 'He held, too, in his enlightened way, that Americans have a perfect right to exist. But he did often find himself wishing Mr. Rhodes had not

enabled them to exerise that right in Oxford'. — In which famous novel about Oxford do these lines occur?

(a) *Tom Brown at Oxford* by T.Hughes(b) *Keddy -A Story of Oxford* by H.N. Dickinson (c) *Sinister Street* by Compton Mackenzie (d) *Zuleika Dobson* by Max Beerbohm

641. Critics often become testy as a result of having to read too many mediocre or bad books. Who wrote about a book : 'This is not a novel to be tossed aside lightly. It should be thrown with great force'?

(a) Doris Lessing (b) Marghanita Laski (c) Bernard Levin (d) Dorothy Parker

642. About literary editors who said, sadly, 'No passion in the world is equal to the passion to alter someone else's draft'?

(a) George Orwell (b) H.G. Wells (c) George Bernard Shaw (d) Ernest Hemingway

643. Who wrote, 'In India', said the nun. . . 'the work of Mr. Eliot is very much respected; he is translated; and many people have written his thesis for his doctorate on inclinations of his work'?

(a) V.S. Naipaul in *An Area of Darkness* (b) Ved Mehta in *Face to Face* (c) Dom Moraes in *My Son's Father* (d) Malcolm Bradbury in *Eating People Is Wrong*

644. Who is the author of this celebrated credo of the

Stream of Consciousness fiction? 'Life is not a series of gig lamps symmetrically arranged; life is a luminious halo, a semi-transparent envelope surrounding us from the beginning of consciousness to the end'.
(a) Dorothy Richardson (b) James Joyce (c) Virginia Woolf (d) Marcel Proust

645. In which novel does this statement occur?
'All animals are equal, but some animals are more equal.'
(a) *The Gulag Archipelago* (b) *Darkness at Noon*
(c) *Animal Farm* (d) *The Castle*

646. 'Barkis is willin'. In which novel is he willing?
(a) *Pamela* (b) *Moll Flanders* (c) *David Copperfield*
(d) *Under the Greenwood Tree*

647. 'Sir Roderick Glossop... is always called a nerve specialist, because it sounds better, but everybody knows that he's really a sort of janitor to the looney-bin.' Whose fiction is repeatedly enriched by this character?
(a) P.G. Wodehouse (b) Kingsley Amis (c) Martin Amis (d) J.P. Donleavy

648. Who wrote 'There's no sweeter tobacco comes from Virginia, and no better brand than Three Castles'?
(a) Winston Churchil (b) Thomas Carlyle (c) W.M. Thackeray (d) Thomas Hardy

649. Home truth from a novelist celebrated for his advocacy of the natural life (whatever that may mean): 'A man with his belly full of classics is an enemy of the human race'. Who is he?
(a) Saul Bellow (b) Arthur Miller (c) Henry Miller (d) Philip Roth

650. What is a trasky novel?
(a) One written like Betty Trask's novels (b) Too risqué (c) Trashy novel with a pleasant ending (d) A combination of traditional and romantic

651. Who was the first woman novelist of England?
(a) Mrs. Aphra Behn (b) Mrs. Anne Radcliffe (c) Charlotte Reade (d) Anne Bradstreet

652. Which American Jewish novelist recently got the Nobel Prize for—Peace?
(a) S.Y. Agnon (b) Bernard Malamud (c) Elie Wiesel (d) Saul Bellow

653. Who is the winner of the 1989 Booker Prize?
(a) Junichiro Tanizaki (b) Salman Rushdie (c) Kazuo Ishiguro (d) Peter Carey

654. How long did Robinson Crusoe have to live in the deserted island in Defoe's novel?
(a) 12 years to a day (b) 16 years (c) 21 years and 4 months (d) 28 years and 2 months

655. Who really is John Le Carré?

(a) Alexander Nesbitt (b) George Horatio Derby
(c) David Cornwell (d) Augustus Fink-Nottle

656. One of the following authors was not a government spy, full-time or part-time. Who?
(a) Christopher Marlowe (b) Daniel Defoe
(c) Graham Greene (d) Malcolm Lowry

657. *Brighton Rock* is the name of Graham Greene's famous early novel. What is Brighton Rock?
(a) A geological specimen (b) A rocky promontory
(c) A pub (d) A sweet made in long, hard sticks

658. Whose detective is Lord Peter Wimsey?
(a) Raymond Chandler (b) Patricia Highsmith
(c) Dorothy L. Sayers (d) Margery Allingham

659. Match the authors with their bestsellers (and what bestsellers! each having sold nine million copies plus):
1.Grace Metalious (a) *Jonathan Livingstone Seagull*
2. Erich Segal (b) *The Exorcist* 3. Richard Bach
(c) *Love Story* 4. William Blatty (d) *Peyton Place*

660. Compared to the earlier list, these are poor bestsellers, four million-plus class. Match the authors with their books:
1. Jacqueline Susan (a) *Rosemary's Baby* 2. Ira Levin
(b) *The Love Machine* 3. Alvin Toffler (c) *Thunderball*
4. Ian Fleming (d) *Future Shock*

661. In perspective, these just about qualify as bestsellers, having sold only two million copies plus (where Spock's *Baby and Child Care* has sold twenty-three million copies plus). Identify the book each author wrote.
1. Pierre Boule (a) *Sanctuary* 2. James Herriott (b) *The Bridge on the River Kwai* 3. James Baldwin (c) *All Things Bright and Beautiful* 4. William Faulkner (d) *Another Country*

662. *Wandering, Journey to the East, Rosshalde* are some of the books by this author who wrote a book on Indian characters which was later filmed. Who is he?
(a) Larry Collins (b) J.G. Ballard (c) Hermann Hesse (d) Aldous Huxley

663. For four years running, 1977-80, this author had one or more of his books on the British bestsellers' list (among the first six). Who is he?
(a) Harold Robbins (b) James Herriot (c) Jack Higgins (d) John Le Carré

664. Match the authors' names with their pen names.
1. Mary Ann Cross (a) Stendhal 2. Marie Henri Beyle (b) Sholom Aleichem 3. Solomon Rabinovich (c) Currer Bell 4. Charlotte Bronte (d) George Eliot

665. 'Mr. Henry James writes fiction as if it were a painful duty'—a critic said. Who?

(a) George Bernard Shaw (b) Oscar Wilde
(c) Virginia Woolf (d) F.R. Leavis

666. Alain Resnais, a gifted French filmmaker, shot into
fame with *Hiroshima mon amour*. Which French
novelist wrote the screenplay?
(a) Alain Robe-Grillet (b) Marguerite Duras
(c) Jean Cayrol (d) Jean Cocteau

667. Who wrote the perennial children's classic *Swiss
Family Robinson* ?
(a) Charles Perrault (b) Louisa May Alcott (c) J.D.
Wyss (d) Carlo Collodi

668. Who wrote the popular French novel *Gigi?*
(a) Louis Ferdinand Celine (b) Amiel (c) Prosper
Merimee (d) Colette

669. A popular novelist once wrote, 'I never read any
novels except my own. When I feel worried,
agitated or upset, I read one and find the last pages
soothe me and leave me happy'. Who?
(a) Barbara Cartland (b) Jacqueline Susan (c) Robin
Cook (d) Harold Robbins

670. 'Some said, "John, print it"; others said, "Not so'.
Some said, "It might do good"; others said, "No".'
— Which John is this?
(a) John Cleland of *Fanny Hill* (b) John Stuart Mill
of *The Subjugation of Women* (c) John Keats of
Endymion (d) John Bunyan of *Pilgrim's Progress*

671. Perhaps the best study of indolence was written by Ivan Aleksandrovich Goncharov, a Russian writer, in 1859. Which is it?
(a) *Rudin* (b) *Oblomov* (c) *A Nest of Gentlefolk* (d) *An Ordinary Story*

672. Charles Dickens was born in
(a) London (b) Dover (c) Portsmouth (d) Bombay

673. Whose detective is Philip Marlowe?
(a) Dorothy L. Sayers (b) Dashiell Hammett (c) Joseph Conrad (d) Raymond Chandler

674. How many copies of Jacqueline Susan's *Valley of the Dolls* could have been sold by now?
(a) 3,750,000 + (b) 10,000,000 + (c) 18, 000, 000 + (d) 26,000, 000 +

675. How many stories does Boccaccio's *Decameron* contain ?
(a) 87 (b) 93 (c) 100 (d) 116

676. Which was the first D.H. Lawrence book to be banned in England?
(a) *Women in Love* (b) *Lady Chatterley's Lover* (c) *John Thomas and Lady Jane* (d) *The Rainbow*

677. In which country was Boris Pasternak's *Doctor Zhivago* first published?
(a) U.S.S.R. (b) France (c) U.S.A. (d) Italy

678. All of Ernest Hemingway's novels were burnt in one country in the 1930s. Which country?
(a) Soviet Russia (b) India (c) Poland (d) Nazi Germany

679. Which was Agatha Christie's first published detective story ?
(a) *The Mysterious Affair at Styles* (b) *The Murder of Roger Ackroyd* (c) *Ten Little Niggers* (d) *Murder on the Orient Express*

680. Which is the first Inspector Maigret book by Simenon?
(a) *Maigret Mystified* (b) *Inspector Maigret Investigates* (c) *Maigret's Rival* (d) *Maigret at the Crossroads*

681. When was Dr Zhivago first published?
(a) 1950 (b) 1957 (c) 1960 (d) 1964

682. Of the following bestselling authors, who is the top of the pop?
(a) Robin Cook (b) Frederick Forsyth (c) Harold Robbins (d) Barbara Cartland

683. '"What's your real name now?"
"George Peters, mum."
"Well, try to remember it, George. Don't forget and tell me it's Elexander before you go, and then get out by saying it's George-Elexander when I catch you."'

Where does this dialogue occur?
(a) *Saturday Night and Sunday Morning* (b) *Nicholas Nickleby* (c) *The Adventures of Huckleberry Finn* (d) *Treasure Island*

684. Which children's story-writer created Paddington Bear?
(a) A.A. Milne (b) Michael Bond (c) Kenneth Grahame (d) Beatrix Potter

685. Match the authors with the books which one is supposed to have read by the time one has finished school.
1. James Fennimore Cooper (a) *Little Women* 2. John R. Wyss (b) *The Deerslayer* 3. Edward Bulwer-Lytton (c) *The Swiss Family Robinson* 4. Louisa May Alcott (d) *The Last Days of Pompeii*

686. This South African novelist, whose work is concerned with the political situation of the country including its apartheid and censorship, wrote *A Guest of Honour, The Conservationist* and *July's People,* among others. Who is the novelist?
(a) Alan Paton (b) Nadine Gordimer (c) Dan Jacobson (d) J.M. Coetzee

687. All except one of the following are novels by Saul Bellow. Which isn't ?
(a) *The Victim* (b) *Seize the Day* (c) *The Rain Came* (d) *Dangling Man*

688. Author of *Adventures of Augie March* and *Henderson the Rain King*, Saul Bellow was the Nobel Prize-winner in 1976. Identify his book from the following :
(a) *Dubins's Lives* (b) *Free Fall* (c) *Jake's Thing* (d) *The Bellarosa Connection*

689. One of this author's books on an Indian theme is considered to be important by many. The same author also wrote *The Longest Journey, Room with a View, and Maurice*. Who is the author?
(a) Virginia Woolf (b) John Masters (c) J.G. Farrell (d) E.M. Forster

690. Can you name the American novel in which the hero is fathered by a computer ?
(a) *2001: A Space Odyssey* (b) *Capricorn Games* (c) *Giles Goat-Boy* (d) *Cat's Cradle*

691. John Wyndham was a science fiction writer who wrote the chilling book
(a) *Dr. Who* (b) *The Food of the God* (c) *Frankenstein Unbound* (d) *The Day of the Triffids*

692. Correlate the author and the book:
1. Ian Fleming (a) *Tobacco Road* 2. Philip Roth (b) *Love Without Fear* 3. Erskine Caldwell (c) *Thunderball* 4. Eustace Chesser (d) *Portnoy's Complaint*

693. Can you identify any book by Czeslaw Milosz, the

Polish poet, novelist, and essayist, Nobel Prize winner 1980, in the following list?
(a) *The Rosy Crucifixion* (c) *Playing for Time* (c) *The Issa Valley* (d) *The Creation of the World*

694. *The Secret Diary of Adrian Mole Aged 13 ¾* published in 1982, took children's literature by storm. Who wrote it?
(a) Barbara Townshend (b) Sue Townsend (c) Elinor Glyn (d) Edith Holden

695. Vladimir Nabokov, author of *Lolita*, was a lepidopterist and so was Stapleton of *The Hound of the Baskervilles*. What does lepidopterist mean?
(a) One who speaks and writes a foreign language like his mother tongue (b) A dirty old man (c) One compulsively attracted to girls of pre-puberty age (d) One who studies or collects moths and butterflies

696. Who, among the following, is a science fiction writer?
(a) Richard Aldington (b) Brian Aldiss (c) Martin Amis (d) T.B. Aldrich

697. Three of the following novels are war novels; one is not. Which one?
(a) *The Naked and the Dead* (b) *From Here to Eternity* (c) *Young Lions* (d) *The Last Exit to Brooklyn*

698. *The Seven Pillars of Wisdom* (1935) is a book about
(a) Indian mysticism (b) Quaker ethics (c) The

154

author's Arabian adventures (d) C.M. Doughty's life with the Bedouins

699. In which detective story is the narrator himself the murderer?
(a) *Trent's Last Case* (b) *Lady Killer* (c) *Dial M for Murder* (d) *The Murder of Roger Ackroyd*

700. Andre Gide, French author, who exercised great influence on modern French fiction, was the recipient of the 1947 Nobel Prize in literature. Identify his novel from the list
(a) *The Mandarins* (b) *Reprieve* (c) *The Counterfeiters* (d) *The Rebel*

701. Which is the earliest John Le Carré title ?
(a) *The Spy Who Came in from the Cold* (b) *A Murder of Quality* (c) *Call for the Dead* (d) *The Looking-Glass War*

702. Match the author with the book.
1. Evelyn Waugh (a) *Pnin* 2. Bernard Malamud (b) *Herzog* 3.Saul Bellow (c) *The Assistant* 4. Vladimir Nabokov (d) *Brideshead Revisited*

703. Which four books belong to Lawrence Durrell's *Alexandria Quartet*?
(a) *Justine* (b) *Balthazar* (c) *Tunc* (d) *Mountolive* (e) *Nunquam* (f) *Clea*

704. Vladimir Nabokov, author of *Lolita*, is one of the

most distinguished writers of the English language. However, two of his well-known novels were written in his mother tongue, Russian. Which?
(a) *Pale Fire* (b) *Pnin* (c) *Despair* (d) *Invitation to a Beheading*

705. Which of the following novels is by John Barth, the American novelist?
(a) *Mr. Sammler's Planet* (b) *Dubin's Lives* (c) *The Sot-Weed Factor* (d) *The Centaur*

706. An English painter, he distinguished himself by his depiction of high and low social life of his times. Fielding and Smollett were influenced by him, while Dickens acknowledged his debt to this painter for his depiction of low life. Who is the painter?
(a) George Cruikshank (b) Joshua Reynolds (c) William Hogarth (d) H.K. Browne (Phiz)

707. A situation of deadlock, composed of two mutually exclusive sets of conclusions — that is the theme of a war novel whose name has contributed a new word to the language. Which among the following is it ?
(a) *Orr's Dilemma* (b) *Catch-22* (c) *Either/Or, Neither* (d) *Logic Feast*

708. Who is the author of *Arabian Nights?*
(a) al-Masudi (b) Nur-al-Nihar (c) Ja'far al-

Barmeki (d) None of the above

709. Sidney, Jim, Lawyer Thatcher, and Joe Harper—
Which book do these characters belong to?
(a) *Oliver Twist* (b) *Lucky Jim* (c) *The Tale of Peter Rabbit* (d) *The Adventures of Tom Sawyer*

710. *Portnoy's Complaint*, a record of the hero's confessions to his psychiatrist, scandalized the readers even as late as 1965. Who is the author?
(a) Philip Roth (b) Saul Bellow (c) Willian Styron (d) E.L. Doctorow

711. *The Prelude: Or, Growth of a Poet's Mind* is an autobiographical poem written by (a) Thomas Gray (b) William Goldsmith (c) S. T. Coleridge (d) William Wordsworth

712. Who wrote the Dr. Dolittle books for children?
(a) Kenneth Grahame (b) A.A. Milne (c) Arthur Ransome (d) Hugh Lofting

713. Who wrote *The Catcher in the Rye* ?
(a) F. Scott-Fitzgerald (b) J.D. Salinger (c) Francis Brett-James (d) Joseph Heller

714. The author of *Guy Mannering, Old Mortality, The Bride of Lammermoor,* and *A Legend of Montrose* also wrote one of the following novels. Which?
(a) *Our Mutual Friend* (b) *Ivanhoe* (c) *Two on a Tower* (d) *Pendennis*

715. The principle of procrastinated rape is said to be the ruling one in all the great bestsellers, V.S. Pritchett remarked. Which is the first popular novel to have adopted this principle successfully?
(a) Defoe's *Moll Flanders* (b) Richardson's *Pamela* (c) Fielding's *Tom Jones* (d) Dicken's *Hard Times*

716. 'There are three rules for writing a novel. Unfortunately, no one knows what they are.' Whose conclusion is this?
(a) E.M.Forster (b) Kingsley Amis (c) John Fowles (d) W. Somerset Maugham

717. In which century were the two parts of Cervantes's *Don Quixote* published?
(a) Fourteenth century (b) Early sixteenth century (c) seventeenth century (d) Early eighteenth century

718 Who did André Gide call 'the best novelist in French literature today'?
(a) Jean-Paul Sartre (b) Simone de Beauvoir (c) Georges Simenon (d) Jean Genet

719. Which was the first printed novel in the modern sense?
(a) Boccaccio's *Decameron* (b) Rabelais' *Gargantua and Pantagruel* (c) Apuleius's *The Golden Ass* (d) Cervantes's *Don Quixote*

720. Who was the first to deal with the Outsider theme?

(a) Albert Camus (b) Jean-Paul Sartre (c) Colin Wilson (d) Jack Kerouac

721. On reading a popular novel, characterized by 'sententious hypocrisy', Henry Fielding was urged to write a parody, *Shamela Andrews*. Which book was he parodying?
(a) *Joseph Andrews* (b) *Pamela Richardson* (c) *Pamela* (d) *The Virtuous Virgin*

722. An American novelist, he made quite a literary reputation in the twenties as a devastating portrayer and satirist of the conformist middle-class American life. In 1930 he was awarded the Nobel Prize in literature. Who is he?
(a) Sinclair Lewis (b) Upton Sinclair (c) Jack London (d) Henry James

723. John Wain created the Angry Young Man, in one of the following novels. Which?
(a) *Room at the Top* (b) *Lucky Jim* (c) *Eating People Is Wrong* (d) *Hurry on Down*.

724. Two of her unfinished novels are *The Watsons*, and *Sanditon*. Who is the novelist?
(a) Charlotte Bronte (b) George Eliot (c) Jane Austen (d) Aphra Behn

725. George Cruikshank (1792-1878) was a famous illustrator and caricaturist, who illustrated the works of many of his distinguished contem-

poraries. However, his fame is associated with one major novelist. Who?
(a) Henry Fielding (b) Samuel Richardson (c) George Borrow (d) Charles Dickens

726. Some of the following authors wrote only one novel. Who?
(a) Charlotte Bronte (b) Emily Bronte (c) Samuel Johnson (d) Samuel Richardson

727. Who on earth is Glumdalclitch?
(a) A character in *Oliver Twist* (b) A character in *Gulliver's Travels* (c) A character in *Roderick Random* (d) A character in *Lavengro*

728 One of E.M. Forster's books, a novel with a homosexual theme, was only published in 1971, a year after Forster's death. Which is it?
(a) *The Longest Journey* (b) *The Celestial Omnibus* (c) *The Hill of Devi* (d) *Maurice*

729. J.P. Donleavy, Irish novelist, has written quite a few novels with alliterative titles. Which of the following are his?
(a) *The Beastly Beatitudes of Balthazar B* (b) *The Porcine Peccadillos of Peregrine Pickle* (c) *The Saddest Summer of Samuel S* (d) *The Loves and Lullabys of Lil Lizzie*

730. Nikita Khrushchev helped Alexander Solzhenitsyn publish one of his books in Soviet Russia.

Which one ?
(a) *One Day in the Life of Ivan Denisovich* (b) *First Circle* (c) *Cancer Ward* (d) *Matryona's Home and Other Stories*

731. The phenomenon of spontaneous combustion so intrigued Dickens that he put it in one of his novels. Which?
(a) *Martin Chuzzlewit* (b) *Our Mutual Friend* (c) *Little Dorrit* (d) *Bleak House*

732. Ascribe the right locale to the right author.
1. Salinus, Calif. (a) Saul Bellow 2. 'Jefferson', Miss. (b) Nathaniel Hawthorne 3. Salem, Mass. (c) John Steinbeck 4. Chicago, Ill. (d) William Faulkner

733. Who introduced the stream of conscionsness mode of fiction writing?
(a) James Joyce (b) Dorothy Richardson (c) Edouard Dujardin (d) Virginia Woolf

734. A trilogy about Harry Angstrom, ex-basketball champion — *Rabbit, Run; Rabbit Redux;* and *Rabbit Is Rich* — the author is known besides for *Couples,* 'a portrait of sexual passion and realignment amongst a group of suburban married couples'. Who is he?
(a) E.L. Doctorow (b) Erica Jong (c) John Updike (d) Harold Robbins

735. What is the nationality of Mario Vargas Llosa, some

of whose novels are: *The Time of the Hero,
Conversations in the Cathedral,* and *The Green House?*
(a) Spanish (b) Italian (c) Mexican (d) Peruvian

736. During the Second World War the German city of
Dresden was completely destroyed by
firebombing. Which novel is set against this
background ?
(a) *The Young Lions* (b) *Catch-22* (c) *Last Waltz in
Dresden* (d) *Slaughterhouse-5*

737. Known best as the author of *the Aunt's Story,Voss,*
and the *Vivisector,* this Australian   novelist was
awarded the Nobel Prize for literature in 1973. Who
is he?
(a) Judith Wright (b) Patrick White (c) Thomas
Kenneally (d) James McAulay

738. It is the story of Hetty Sorrel, pretty, vain, and self-
centred. She is loved by the village carpenter, but
falls for the young Squire Arthur Donnithorne,
who gets her with child and abandons her. So far,
the story is nothing out of the ordinary. It is only
after the girl kills the newborn baby that the
seriousness of the novel is slowly revealed. It is an
English classic, but which is it?
(a) *Adam Bede* (b) *The Heart of Midlothian* (c) *Tess of
the D'Urbervilles* (d) *Oliver Twist*

739. In recent times, which science fiction author has
been the most creative in promoting SF as a literary

genre? To give you a tip, he wrote *Moreau's Other Island*.
(a) Isaac Asimov (b) Brian Aldiss (c) Arthur C. Clarke (d) Michael Moorcock

740. Which British Prime Minister was a distinguished novelist as well?
(a) Lord Palmerstone (b) Harold Wilson (c) Benjamin Disraeli (d) Harold Macmillan

741. *The Mask of Dimitrios* (1939) is a spy novel, pronounced to be of a very high order. Who is the author?
(a) John Le Carré (his Le always has an uppercase L) (b) Eric Ambler (c) Dashiell Hammett (d) Martin Cruz-Smith

742. Who are the three musketeers in the novel of the same name by Alexandre Dumas?
(a) Hector, Hestor, and Nestor (b) Athos, Porthos, and Aramis (c) Jean, Louis, and Karl (d) Artemidorus, Polybus, and Croesus

743. He is one of the most prominent 'New Wave' science fiction writers and wrote such books as *The Drowned World* and *High Rise*. He has recently turned away from science fiction and written a bestselling war novel set in China. Identify him.
(a) Brian Aldiss (b) Michael Moorcock (c) Arthur C. Clarke (d) J.G. Ballard

744. In which book of Swift's *Gulliver's Travels* does the country or Balnibarbi find a mention?
(a) Liliput (b) Brobdingnag (c) Laputa (d) Houyhnhnms

745. Who, among the following Arthurian Knights, succeeds in recovering the Holy Grail?
(a) Sir Galahad (b) Sir Gawain (c) Sir Launcelot (d) King Arthur

746. Among the Beat Generation writers, the poets, like Allen Ginsberg, Gregory Corso, and Lawrence Ferlinghetti attained great fame, but the novelists are less talked about. Who among the following are Beat novelists?
(a) Henry Miller (b) Willian Burroughs (c) John Clellon Holmes (d) Philip Roth

747. A French novelist and essayist of existentialist persuasion, her books include *The Mandarins* and *The Second Sex*. She died recently. Who is she?
(a) Germaine Greer (b) Simone de Beauvoir (c) Harriet Martineau (d) Simone Weil

748. Who was it who survived with King Arthur the last battle against Modred and bore the King to the barge which bore him away to Avalon?
(a) Merlin (b) Sir Launcelot (c) Sir Gawain (d) Sir Bedevere

749 In which play do the characters Peachum, Polly,

Lockit, Lucy, and Captain Macheath appear?
(a) *Beggar's Opera* (b) *The Threepenny Opera* (c) *Peter Grimes* (d) *Vanessa*

750. Although he wrote fourteen novels in all, his fame rests solely on *Lorna Doone* (1867). Who is this late-Victorian novelist?
(a) William Cullen Bryant (b) Algernon Blackwood (c) R.D. Blackmore (d) T.E. Browne

751. A Gothic novel is filled with ghosts, vaults, giants, living statues, mysterious appearances, and violent emotions of love, terror, and anguish. Who wrote the first true Gothic novel?
(a) Horace Walpole (b) Monk Lewis (c) Mrs Beckford (d) Mrs Radcliffe

752. Can you relate the following Dickensian characters with the right books?
1. Dr Chillip (a) *Nicholas Nickleby* 2. Cherry and Merry (b) *Bleak House* 3. Cheeryble Brothers (c) *David Copperfield* 4. Chadband (d) *Martin Chuzzlewit*

753. For writing *Fanny Hill,* John Cleland was summoned before the Privy Council on the charge of indecency. What was the outcome?
(a) He was pilloried (b) Fined £5000, and the copies of the book burnt (c) Sentenced to two years hard labour (d) He was discharged

754. Can you say who wrote *Fire on the Mountain, Clear Light of Day, Games at Twilight,* and *The Village by the Sea?*
(a) Anita Desai (b) James Baldwin (c) Iris Murdoch (d) V.S. Naipaul

755. 'Pray, my dear,' quoth my mother, 'have you not forgot to wind up the clock?' This famous interruption in an act of creation occurs in an eighteenth century novel. Which?
(a) Smollett, *Roderick Random* (b) Defoe, *Moll Flanders* (c) Sterne, *Tristram Shandy* (d) Richardson, *Pamela*

756. Bartoline Saddletree, the Captain of Knock-dunder, Douce Davie Deans and Meg Murdockson are some of the minor characters in this novel. Which is it?
(a) *Bleak House* by Dickens (b) *Pendennis* by Thackeray (c) *The Heart of Midlothian* by Scott (d) *Moll Flanders* by Defoe

757. 'It was as true', said ... , ' as taxes is. And nothing's truer than them.' Said who?
(a) Joe Gargery of *Great Expectations* (b) Barkis of *David Copperfield* (c) Mr. Squeers of *Nicholas Nickleby* (d) Sam Waller of *The Pickwick Papers*

758. Ann Radcliffe's name is known to the students of the history of English literature, though not many of them may have read her *Mysteries of Udolphe*.

Why is the novel important?
(a) As the first English novel touching on the subject of sex, albeit covertly (b) As a super ghost story (c) As among the first Gothic Romances (d) As the first historical novel (1794), long before Scott established the genre.

759. H.K. Browne (Phiz) was a famous nineteenth century illustrator of books. His name is associated with a novelist of his time. Which?
(a) Jane Austen (b) Charles Dickens (c) George Meredith (d) Thomas Hardy

760. In which novel of Dickens does one find the Artful Dodger ?
(a) *Oliver Twist* (b) *Old Curiosity Shop* (c) *Nicholas Nickleby* (d) *Martin Chuzzlewit*

761. A young lady turns up in Boston with a baby in her arms. She refuses to name her lover, is pilloried, and sentenced to wear the red letter A for Adultress for the rest of her life. In which novel does one find her?
(a) *The Sinful Mistress* (b) *Suffering in Boston* (c) *The Scarlet Letter* (d) *The Ordeals of Hester Prynne*

762. *A Man Lay Dead, Died in the Wool* and *Final Curtain* are some of the detective stories of Dame Ngaio Marsh, a New Zealander. How does one pronounce her christian name?
(a) Ny-o (b) En-gai-o (c) Engo (d) En-gao

763. This lady sued Dickens's Mr. Pickwick for breach of promise. Who is she?
(a) Mrs. Gummidge (b) Mrs. Lirriper (c) Mrs. Bardell (d) Mrs. Cluppins

764. Which is the first Conan Doyle book in which Holmes and Watson collaborate?
(a) *The Hound of the Baskervilles* (b) *The White Company* (c) *A Study in Scarlet* (d) *The Lost World*

765. Match the authors' names with their pen names.
1. Francois Thibault (a) Maxim Gorky 2. William Sidney Porter (b) O. Henry 3. Alexie Peishkov (c) Katherine Mansfield 4. Kathleen Beauchamp (d) Anatole France

766. Who wrote *The Last of the Mohicans?*
(a) Bret Harte (b) Theodore Dreiser (c) Harriet Beecher Stowe (d) James Fennimore Cooper

767. Match the author with the book:
1. H. Rider Haggard (a) *Ben-Hur* 2. Anna Sewell (b) *Three Men in a Boat* 3. Jerome K. Jerome (c) *She* 4. Lew Wallace (d) *Black Beauty*

768. 'Who reads Marie Corelli today?' Perhaps few. She was Queen Victoria's favourite novelist, which tells one something about her novels. Can you identify a Corelli novel in the list?
(a) *She* (b) *Thelma* (c) *Pamela* (d) *Sorrows of Werther*

769. This novel was described by T.S Eliot as 'the first, the longest and the best detective story'. Choose the right book.
(a) Conan Doyle's *The Hound of the Baskervilles* (b) Wilkie Collins's *The Moonstone* (c) Charles Dickens's *Bleak House* (d) William Godwin's *Caleb Williams*

770. Match the characters with the books:
1. George Wickham (a) *Persuasion* 2. Frank Churchill (b) *Mansfield Park* 3. Frederick Wentworth (c) *Pride and Projudice* 4. Fanny Price *Emma*

771. Tolstoy's *War and Peace* is a truly monumental work of fiction of 700,000 words and a very large number of characters. Can you guess how many?
(a) 138 (b) 262 (c) A few less than 400 (d) 539

772. Angus Wilson takes the title of his book *Anglo-Saxon Attitudes* from a famous book. Which is it?
(a) *Anglo-Saxon Chronicles* (b) *England Made Me* (c) *Through the Looking Glass* (d) *Don Juan*

773. Voltaire's major work was *The Age of Louis XIV*. However, he wrote two philosophical tales, one of which was *Candide*. Which is the other?
(a) *Vathek* (b) *The Gates of Summer* (c) *Zadig* (d) *Mount of Olives*

774. Maggie Tulliver, Stephen Guest, Mr Glegg, and

Wakem are characters in a George Eliot novel. Can you name which?
(a) *Adam Bede* (b) *The Mill on the Floss* (c) *Silas Marner* (d) *Middlemarch*

775. *The Newgate Calendar*, published in many editions, but the first such in 1773, recorded notorious crimes from 1700 up to date. Can you identify from the following list a novel which was indebted to it?
(a) Dickens's *Oliver Twist* (b) Thackeray's *Pendennis* (c) Hardy's *Tess of the D'Urbervilles* (d) Defoe's *Colonel Jack*

776. Match the authors with their books.
(1) Ray Bradbury (a) *Act of Will* (2) Barbara Taylor Bradford (b) *Fanny* (3) Erica Jong (c) *Fahrenheit 451* (4) Len Deighton (d) *Spy Hook*

777. His greatest novel has been called 'the closest approach the United States has had to a national prose epic', although in his lifetime he suffered the misfortunes of censorship, misunderstanding and neglect. Who is the author whose other works include *Omoo*, *Redburn*, and *White Jacket*?
(a) Richard Henry Dana (b) Nathaniel Hawthorne (c) Herman Melville (d) Henry David Thoreau

778. In 1973 a picaresque novel of sex and psychiatry, *Fear of Flying*, was published and even on such a late date created a sensation. Who wrote it?
(a) Philip Roth (b) Germaine Greer (c) Erica Jong

(d) Desmond Morris

779. *The Wonderful Story of Henry Sugar* is a delightful children's tale by a writer famous for his macabre stories. Who is he?
(a) Patricia Highsmith (b) John Wyndham (c) Nicholas Freeling (d) Roald Dahl

780. The author of *Singular Man*, *Leila*, and *Schultz* is
(a) Saul Bellow (b) J.P. Donleavy (c) J.D. Salinger (d) John Updike

781. He is well known as the author of sea stories, and wrote the Hornblower series. Who is he?
(a) Herman Melville (b) Joseph Conrad (c) C.S. Forester (d) Ernest Hemingway

782. Her novels have titles like *Death in*, among other places, *The Andamans*, *Berlin*, *Cyprus*, *Kashmir*, *Kenya and Zanzibar*. She has also written a very popular romance on India. Who is the author?
(a) Monica Dickens (b) Ivy Compton-Burnett (c) M.M. Kaye (d) Doris Lessing

783. Who is the author of the autobiography *A Sort of Life*?
(a) Aldous Huxley (b) Kingsley Amis (c) Graham Greene (d) P.G. Wodehouse

784. An author of much science fiction, he wrote in 1984 a novel about his own war-time experiences called

Empire of the Sun. Who could he be?
(a) Brian Aldiss (b) Isaac Asimov (c) J.G. Ballard
(d) Michael Moorcock

785. Who wrote the modern classic *The Tin Drun*?
(a) Gunter Grass (b) Arthur Hailey (c) James Hadley Chase (d) Susan Howatch

786. 'Gargantuan' (appetite) derives from the classic *Gargantua and Pantagruel.* Who wrote it?
(a) Boccaccio (b) Cervantes (c) Rabelais (d) Aretino

787. *Autumn of the Patriarch, Innocent Erendira, Leaf Sorm, In Evil Hour*—the list does not include the most famous of the author's novels. Which is it?
(a) *Adam, One Afternoon* (b) *Nothing, Doting, Blindness* (c) *The Crying of Lot 49* (d) *One Hundred Years of Solitude*

788. *Hunger, Growth of the Soil, Pan* are some of his more famous novels. who is he?
(a) Mikhail Sholokhov (b) Ignazio Silone (c) Knut Hamsun (d) Alexander Solzhenitsyn

789. Which among the following is not a Graham Greene novel?
(a) *England Made Me* (b) *The Power and the Glory*
(c) *The Heart of Africa* (d) *The Honorary Consul*

790. This novel, offered to publishers in 1944, was considered too hot to handle by, among others,

Victor Gollancz, Faber and Faber, Jonathan Cape; ultimately Secker and Warburg published it. Which novel is it?

(a) *Darkness at Noon* (b) *The God that Failed* (c) *Animal Farm* (d) *Lolita*

791. Who is the author of *The Gulag Archipelago?*
(a) Martin Cruz Smith (b) Alexander Solzhenitsyn (c) Andrei Voznesensky (d) Israel Zangwill

792. Twenty years after he published *Thirty-nine Steps,* he was made governor general of Canada. Who was he?
(a) Frank Buchanan (b) John Buchan (c) James Buchanan (d) Beau Brummell

793. An employee of a book wholesaler, Rene Raymond, assumed a literary name and became a celebrated author of sex and violence fiction. Who is he?
(a) Jack Higgins (b) Robert Ludlum (c) Harold Robbins (d) James Hadley Chase

794. How many Bond books did Ian Fleming write?
(a) 10 (b) 13 (c) 16 (d) 21

795. Who is the author of *A House for Mr. Biswas?*
(a) R.K. Narayan (b) Raja Rao (c) V.S. Naipaul (d) Manohar Malgonkar

796. Who is the author of *Quo Vadis,* a novel about

Christianity in the Roman emperor Nero's time?
(a) Alexandre Dumas (b) Sholom Aleichem
(c) Walecz Korzeniwosky (d) Henrik Sienkiewicz

797. Can you identify a book by a Nobel Prize winning author among the following?
(a) *The Tenant* (b) *Ulysses* (c) *The Hot Gates* (d) *The Power and the Glory*

798. Graham Greene was once on a two-year contract with Metro-Goldwyn-Mayer, and wrote for them a story in 1944 which lay in their archives, unused and forgotten. It was recovered in 1983, revised by Greene, and published in 1985. Which is the novel?
(a) *Dr. Fischer and the Bomb Party* (b) *The Captain and the Enemy* (c) *The Tenth Man* (d)*The Third Man*

799. In naming his characters, Dickens seems to have a particular preference for the letter J: Mrs Jiniwin, Alfred Jingle, Mrs Jaggers, Mrs Jorley, John Jarndyce, Miss Jellyby, Jo, Joe, Job Trotter, Joe Gargery, Mr Jorkins, Sissy Jupe—are some examples. Can you identify some of the following with the books they come from?
1. Mrs Jellyby (a) *Hard Times* 2. Joe Gargery (b) *David Copperfield* 3. Cissy Jupe (c) *Bleak House* 4. Mr Jorkins (d) *Great Expectations*

800. Marlow is the part-narrator of several of Joseph Conrad's novels. Which, among the following?
(a) *Lord Jim* (b) *Heart of Darknes* (c) *Nostromo*

(d) *Youth*

801. 'The Monkey's Paw' is a macabre story dramatized very successfully, more known in the dramatic form than as a story. Who wrote it?
(a) H.H. Munro (Saki) (b) W.W. Jacobs (c) A.A. Milne (d) Jean Rhys

802. Identify the book in which the following Dickensian characters appear.
1. Guppy (a) *The Old Curiosity Shop* 2. Sir Mulberry Hawk (b) *Pickwick Papers* 3. Mrs. Jiniwin (c) *Nicholas Nickleby* 4. Alfred Jingle (d) *Bleak House*

803. Who wrote the alarming novel of violence *A Clockwork Orange*, which was made into a film by Stanley Kubrick in 1971?
(a) John Berger (b) Guy Burgess (c) Anthony Burgess (d) William Burroughs

804. This unfortunate girl failed to get married in a Hardy novel because she went to the wrong church. Who is she?
(a) Sue in *Jude the Obscure* (b) Elizabeth in *Mayor of Casterbridge* (c) Marian in *Tess of the D'Urbervilles* (d) Fanny in *Far from the Madding Crowd*

805. Who wrote *The Ginger Man*?
(a) Barbara Taylor Bradford (b) Sean O'Casey (c) Sean O'Faolain (d) J.P. Donleavy

806. *A Group of Noble Dames, The Well-Beloved, The Hand of Ethelberta,* and *Desperate Remedies* are some of the less frequently read novels of this famous novelist. Who is he?

(a) W.M. Thackeray (b) Thomas Hardy (c) Sir Walter Scott (d) Charlotte Bronte

807. The *Wilhelm Meister* trilogy became the prototype of German novel of character development. Who wrote it?

(a) Friedrich von Schiller (b) Friedrich Durrenmatt (c) Johann Wolfgang von Goethe (d) Thomas Mann

808. Who wrote *The Horse's Mouth,* a novel about the artist Gulley Jimson?

(a) Irving Stone (b) Aldous Huxley (c) James Joyce (d) Joyce Cary

809 He is not an American Jewish, but Israeli novelist and has written books like *Elsewhere Perhaps* and *My Michael* - on contemporary Israeli life. Who is he?

(a) Isaac Bashevis Singer (b) Chaim Potok (c) Bruno Levi (d) Amos Oz

810. Match the authors with books.

1. Doris Lessing (a) *The Confederacy of Dunces* 2. John Barth (b) *Mosquito Coast* 3. John Kennedy Toole (c) *The Golden Notebook* 4. Paul Theroux (d) *Giles Goat-Boy*

811. Julius and Ethel Rosenberg, convicted and executed in the U.S. in 1953 in an espionage case, form the background of a novel by E.L. Doctorow, Which is it?
(a)*Ragtime* (b) *Loon Lake* (c) *The Book of Daniel* (d) *The Public Burning*

812. Match the characters with the books:
1. Brett Ashley (a) *1984* 2. Catherine Barkley (b) *The Great Gatsby* 3. Rubashov (c) *Fiesta* or *The Sun Also Rises* 4. Daisy Buchanan (d) *A Farewell to Arms*

813. *The Flounder, From the Diary of a Snail, The Meeting at Telgte,* are some of his later works; but this German novelist (born in Danzig) burst upon the literary scene in 1959 with a novel about the Nazi regime and the war. What is the novel and who is the author?
(a) Uwe Johnson (b) Hans Bender (c) Gunter Grass (d) Peter Weiss

814. *Getting to Know the General, In Search of a Character, A Sort of Life,* and *The Captain and the Enemy* are admittedly the lesser known works of this novelist. Who is he?
(a) Graham Greene (b) Anthony Powell (c) John Cowper Powys (d) John Fowles

815. The Stonehenge, a group of standing stones on Salisbury Plain, in Wiltshire, England, features prominently in an important English novel.

Which is it?

(a) Fielding's *Tom Jones* (b) Scott's *The Heart of Midlothian* (c) Dicken's *Great Expectations* (d) Hardy's *Tess of the D'Urbervilles*

816. Chiron, the wounded centaur, gave his immortality to Prometheus and died. An important modern novel, *The Centaur,* follows the theme. Who wrote it?

(a) Bernard Malamud (b) John Updike (c) William Styron (d) Saul Bellow

817. Nazi concentration camps have provided the material of many post-war novels. This one, perhaps, is the most remarkable of them. Identify it.

(a) E.L. Doctorow's *Loon Lake* (b) Isaac Bashevis Singer's *The Magician of Lublin* (c) William Styron's *Sophie's Choice* (d) Chaim Potok's *The Chosen*

818. In which of the following books does Joyce's Stephen Dedalus feature?

(a) *Dubliners* (b) *A Portrait of the Artist as a Young Man* (c) *Ulysses* (d) *Finnegans Wake*

819. Among the following novels of Salman Rushdie, which is the earliest?

(a) *Shame* (b) *Midnight's Children* (c) *Grimus* (d) *Satanic Verses*

820. Which is the latest John Le Carré book?

(a) *A Perfect Spy* (b) *The Little Drummer Girl*
(c) *Smiley's People* (d) *The Russia House*

821. Of the following books by John Le Carré which does not feature George Smiley?
(a) *Call for the Dead* (b) *A Murder of Quality* (c) *A Small Town in Germany* (d) *Tinker, Tailor, Soldier, Spy*

822. A man wakes up one morning to find himself transformed into a giant insect: this is how a story, which has now become a classic, begins. Who is the author?
(a) Vladimir Nabokov (b) Franz Kafka (c) Albert Camus (d) Thomas Mann

823. Who wrote the novel *The Ambassadors*?
(a) Henry James (b) Graham Greene (c) Aldous Huxley (d) Lord Curzon

824. From the beginning Bigger was doomed. He was a nigger on Chicago's South Side, and ended on, where else but, the electric chair. Which novel tells his story?
(a) Ralph Ellison's *Invisible Man* (b) Alice Walker's *The Color People* (c) Langston Hughes's *Not Without Laughter* (d) Richard Wright's *Native Son*

825. 'Big Brother is watching you', the caption with the portrait exhibited in every public place, is an unseen character in
(a) *Darkness at Noon* (b) *Gulag Archipelago* (c) *1984*

(d) *Animal Farm*

826. What is the name of G.K. Chesterton's detective ?
(a) Miss Marples (b) Lord Peter Wimsey (c) Father Brown (d) Peter Brown

827. In which book did P.G. Wodehouse first introduce Bertie Wooster and Jeeves?
(a) *Carry on, Jeeves* (b) *The Man with Two Left Feet* (c) *Inimitable Jeeves* (d) *Very Good, Jeeves*

828. Quite a few good novels about the Second World War have been written. Which is the most famous First World War novel?
(a) *Sherston's Progress* by Sigfried Sassoon (b) *Goodbye to All That* by Robert Graves (c) *All Quiet on the Western Front* by Erich Maria Remarque (d) *The Young Lions* by Irwin Shaw

829. This novel is regarded by many as a mirror of the jazz era.
(a) *Catcher in the Rye* (b) *Goodbye to All That* (c) *Last Tycoon* (d) *Great Gatsby*

830. Match the characters with the books.
1. Captain Ahab (a) *Ulysses* 2. Hester Prynne (b) *1984* 3. Buck Mulligan (c) *The Scarlet Letter* 4. Winston (d) *Moby Dick*

831 Match the authors with the books:
1. William Somerset Maugham (a) *For Whom the*

Bell Tolls 2. Ernest Hemingway (b) *Rabbit Run* 3. John Updike (c) *A House for Mr Biswas* 4. V.S. Naipaul (d) *Razor's Edge*

832. Match the author with the book:
1. Harper Lee (a) *Never Love a Stranger* 2. Harold Robbins (b) *Fear of Flying* 3. Erskine Caldwell (c) *To Kill a Mocking Bird* 4. Erica Jong (d) *God's Little Acre*

833. Which is the odd one out ?
(a) *Catcher in the Rye*   (b) *Tender is the Night* (c) *Franny and Zooey* (d) *Raise High the Roofbeam, Carpenters*

834. Of the following titles in John Updike's Rabbit series, which one is bogus?
(a)*Rabbit Run* (b) *Rabbit Redux* (c) *Rabbit on Top* (d) *Rabbit is Rich*

835. V.S. Naipaul is known principally as a novelist, although he has written some travel books, notably *An Area of Darkness*. Which among the following is another travel book of his?
(a) *Finding the Centre* (b) *Miguel Street* (c) *A Turn in the South* (d) *Enigma of Arrival*

836. Shiva Naipaul was V.S. Naipaul's brother and a distinguished novelist. Can you identify one of his books from the following?
(a) *Fireflies* (b) *Guerrillas* (c) *In a Free State* (d) *Mimic Man*

837. Who wrote *Nightmare Abbey* (1818)?
(a) T.L. Peacock (b) Jane Austen (c) Monk Lewis
(d) Mrs. Radcliffe

838. Jorge Luis Borges, Argentine author, whose influence Salman Rushdie acknowledges, is the author of some of the following books. Identify which.
(a) *A Universal History of Infamy* (b) *The Autumn of the Patriarch* (c) *Leaf Storm* (d) *The Book of Sand*

839. The author of *Shadows on the Grass*, *Seven Gothic Tales*, and *Anecdotes of Destiny* also wrote one of the following books which established her reputation. The book was subsequently filmed. Identify the book.
(a) *Out of Africa* (b) *Farewell My Lovely* (c) *Goodbye Mr. Chipps* (d) *Lace*

840. Golding's *Lord of the Flies* is a terrifying vision of the collapse of democratic norms and man's lapse into savagery. Who is the Lord of the flies?
(a) The pig (b) Satan (c) Beelzebub (d) Belial

841. Isaac Bashevis Singer won the Nobel Prize in literature in 1978. Can you identity his works (stories, novels) in the following list?
(a) 'A Crown of Feathers' (b) 'Gimpel the Fool'
(c) 'Pigeon Feathers' (d) *Shosha*

842. A South African novelist, a winner of many literary

prizes, J.M. Coetzee (b. 1940) has still a fruitful future ahead of him. Which among the following novels is his?
(a) *The Life and Times of Michael K* (b) *Dusklands*
(c) *The Barbarians* (d) *In the Heart of the Country*

843. *Cry, the Beloved Country*, published 1948, was one of the earlier novels to have come out of South Africa on the question of races, simply and compassionately told. Who wrote it?
(a) Nadine Gordimer (b) Alan Paton (c) J.M. Coetzee (d) Dan Jacobson

844. Match the author with the book.
1. Aldous Huxley (a) *The Naked and the Dead*
2. Graham Greene (b) *Catcher in the Rye* 3. Norman Mailer (c) *The Power and the Glory* 4. J.D. Salinger (d) *Crome Yellow*

845. In whose novel does Jim Dixon, unsuccessful lecturer in History and angry young man, appear?
(a) Kingsley Amis (b) John Wain (c) John Braine (d) Alan Sillitoe

846. *The Loneliness of the Long-Distance Runner*, the story of a borstal boy, made into a film later, is Alan Sillitoe's novel published in 1959. The previous year he had written a sensational first novel. Which is it?
(a) *The Death of William Posters* (b) *Saturday Night and Sunday Morning* (c) *A Start in Life*

(d) *A Tree on Fire*

847. One of the following is not a Steinbeck novel. Which ?
(a) *The Winter of Our Discontent* (b) *The Cotton Pickers* (c) *The Grapes of Wrath* (d) *In Dubious Battle*

848. Which of the following Wolf/Wolfes wrote *Look Homeward Angel?*
(a) Hugo Wolf (b) Charles Wolfe (c) Reyner Wolfe (d) Thomas Clayton Wolfe

849. Which black American novelist wrote these books: *Giovanni's Room, Going to Meet the Man, If Beale Street Could Talk,* and *Just Above My Head?*
(a) James Baldwin (b) Alice Childress (c) Alex Hailey (d) Langston Hughes

850. *Darkness at Noon* (1941) is a novel about the purge of a deviationist Bolshevik under Stalin's orders, written by a disillusioned communist. Who is he?
(a) George Orwell (b) Arthur Koestler (c) Christopher Caudwell (d) Alexander Solzhenitsyn

851. Identify another book by the author of *Ragtime* from the following list:
(a) *Mr. Sammler's Planet* (b) *The Assistant* (c) *Slaughterhouse -5* (d) *Loon Lake*

852. Ralph Ellison wrote a classic novel detailing the

struggles of a nameless young black man in a hostile society. What is the name of the novel?
(a) *Black Boy* (b) *Native Son* (c) *Another Country* (d) *Invisible Man*

853. William Faulkner, the well-known American novelist of the South, also wrote a moving play. Identify it.
(a) *Light in August* (b) *As I lay Dying* (c) *Absalom, Absalom !* (d) *Requiem for a Nun*

854. Jean Giradoux (1882-1944), a French novelist and dramatist, had one of his plays, perhaps the best known to English readers, translated by Christopher Fry. Which is it?
(a) *The Balcony* (b) *No Exit* (c) *The Tiger at the Gates* (d) *Caligula*

855. Who wrote *The Longest Journey*?
(a) Joseph Conrad (b) E.M. Forster (c) Graham Greene (d) Paul Theroux

856. Haldor Laxness, the Icelander, was awarded the Nobel Prize in 1955 for
(a) reviving an interest in Icelandic sagas (b) his exposition of Taoism (c) his epic novels of rural life (d) his poetry.

857. This book was rejected by two editors. The first died of a heart attack within a month; the second hanged himself from a tree, wearing a bra and

panties. The third editor passed the manuscript and later won the Nobel Prize. Which book is it?
(a) Samuel Beckett's *Endgame* (b) James Joyce's *Stephen Hero* (c) Robert Graves's *The White Goddess* (d) George Orwell's *Animal Farm*

858. *Jerusalem the Golden, The Needle's Eye,* and *The Middle Ground* are some of her novels. She has also edited *The Oxford Companion to English Literature* (1985). Who is she?
(a) Rebecca West (b) Margaret Drabble (c) Iris Murdock (d) Edna O'Brien

859. Henry Miller, author of *Tropic of Cancer,* and *Tropic of Capricorn* (both, alas, banned in India) wrote an excellent travel book on Greece. Which is it?
(a) *The Smiling Sphinx* (b) *The Aegean Isles* (c) *In Homer Country* (d) *The Colossus of Maroussi*

860. *The Garden Of Eden, The Dangerous Summer,* and *The Fifth Column* are some of the books by this American novelist who is famous for some or his other books. Who is he?
(a) Ernest Hemingway (b) William Faulkner (c) Thomas Wolfe (d) John Steinbeck

861. 'Mistah Kurtz—he dead.' This line was used by T.S. Eliot as an epigraph to *The Hollow Men.* Where does it occur?
(a) Dickens :*The Mystery of Edwin Drood* (b) Joseph Conrad : *The Heart of Darkness* (c) Graham Greene:

In Search of a Character   (d) Wole Soyinka : *The Interpreters*

862. Match the characters with the books :
1. Ferguson (a) *Lucky* 2. Jaime (b) *Outbreak*
3. Marissa (c) *The Sands of Time* 4. Gino
(d) *Confessional*

10

RECONDITE REFERENCES

863. Where does one meet the Cheshire Cat?
(a) English nursery rhymes (b) *Winnie the Pooh*
(c) *Alice's Adventures in Wonderland* (d) *The Wind in the Willows*

864. Concord, Massachusetts, is inseparably connected with this author, one of the most important influences on American thought and literature. Who is he?
(a) Mark Twain (b) Ralph Waldo Emerson (c) Stephen Vincent Benet (d) Henry David Thoreau

865. Some of the greatness of Alfred the Great (A.D. 848-99) derives from his patronage of literature. He is remembered for his translation of quite a few Latin texts, but certain great projects were started with his initiative. Can you identify which?
(a) Compilation of the *Domesday Book*
(b) Translation of the Bible into West Saxon
(c) Compilation of the *Anglo-Saxon Chronicle*
(d) Translation of the Homeric epics

866. *Portrait of a Genius, But...* (1950) is a famous, but controversial biography of D.H. Lawrence. This was written by the novelist's close friend. Who is the biographer?
(a) David Garnett (b) Richard Aldington (c) J. Middleton Murry (d) Lady Ottoline Morrell

867. Match the dates with the authors:
1. 1895-1952 (a) Albert Camus 2. 1821-67 (b) Jean-Paul Sartre 3. 1913-60 (c) Charles Baudelaire 4. 1905-80 (d) Paul Eluard

868. Penguin Books reprinted some years ago *Hindoo Holiday*, the impression of an Englishman as private secretary to an Indian Maharaja. Who wrote it?
(a) John Masters (b) J.R. Ackerley (c) Philip Mason (d) Paul Scott

869. A medieval scholar at Oxford, he wrote very popular children's books like *The Hobbit* and *The Lord of the Rings*, which many adults also seem to savour. Who is he?
(a) J.R.R. Tolkien (b) C.S. Lewis (c) J.A.W. Bennett (d) John Burrow

870. What is the source of the expression 'cloud-cuckoo-land'?
(a) Sidney's *Arcadia* (b) More's *Utopia* (c) Aristophanes's *The Birds* (d) Euripides's *Bacchae*

871. Who is the most celebrated Polish writer of English?
(a) Vladimir Nabokov (b) Joseph Conrad (c) Franz Kafka (d) Karl Popper

872. The following English painters influenced literature considerably. Can you arrange their names chronologically?
(a) Hogarth (b) Reynolds (c) Gainsborough (d) Constable

873. In the history of literary movements there have often been revivals of trends of the past. Relate the following revivals to their appropriate authors.
1. Neo-classicism (a) Italo Calvino 2. Neo-realism (b) Pico della Mirandolla 3. Neo-Platonism (c) Petrarch 4. Gothic revival (d) Mrs.Ann Radcliffe

874. The terms Philistine , Barbarian, and the Populace were coined by an English poet and essayist to describe the middle classes, the aristocracy and the working classes, respectively. Who used them?
(a) Dr. Johnson (b) S.T. Coleridge (c) Lord Byron (d) Matthew Arnold

875. 'Man is born free; and everywhere he is in chains.' This statement occurs in a book called *Social Contract*, an important book on the theory of state, and a great influence on English romantic

movement. Who is the author?
(a) Voltaire (b) Rousseau (c) Hobbes (d) Locke

876. About Lord Chesterfield's 'Letters' to his son someone said that 'They teach the morals of a whore and the manners of a dancing master' Who?
(a) Jonathan Swift (b) James Boswell (c) Dr. Johnson (d) F.R. Leavis

877. When was the first authorized version of the Koran prepared?
(a) A.D. 630 (b) A.D. 650 (c) A.D. 817 (d) A.D. 912

878. Match the dates with the English literary movements.
1.1660— (a) Georgian 2. 1603— (b) Romantic
3. 1798— (c) Jacobean 4. 1910— (d) Restoration

879. Samuel Beckett's first novel is *More Pricks Than Kicks*, pricks meaning sharp weapons, and not something else. Where does he get the idea of the title from?
(a) Shakespeare (b) Dante (c) The Bible (d) Joyce

880. Dadaism, which stressed absurdity and the role of the unpredictable in creation, originated with
(a) Salvador Dali (b) Tristan Tsara (c) Max Ernst (d) Marcel Duchamp

881. Who among the following belonged to the

Bloomsbury Group?
(a) Edith Sitwell (b) Virginia Woolf (c) Aldous Huxley (d) E.M. Forster

882. Who coined the critical term 'Objective Correlative'?
(a) William Empson (b) F.R. Leavis (c) I.A. Richards (d) T.S. Eliot

883. The French Revolution and the publication of *The Lyrical Ballads* occurred on dates which are anagrams of each other. Give the dates from the following choices.
(a) 1987 (b) 1877 (c) 1931 (d) 1891

884. Which was the first book of essays to be published?
(a) Bacon's *Essays* (b) Montaigne's *Essais* (c) La Rochefoucauld's *Maxims* (d) Cicero's *De Amicitia*

885. What is Anne Bradstreet distinguished as?
(a) The first American Nobel laureate (b) Winner of the Pulitzer prize for five successive years (c) The first important woman author in America (d) The first woman author whose books were banned in Boston

886. Georgian is a term applied to the writers of the reign of one of the Georges. Which one?
(a) George III (b) George V (c) George VI (d) George VII

887. In 1951 R.H. Crossman edited a volume of essays called *The God That Failed,* which immediately created a lot of controversy. Which God?
(a) The God of the Catholics (b) The God of the *Bhagvad Gita* (c) Democratic Socialism (d) Communism

888. The following are some of the important works of the period. Match them correctly.
1. *Prometheus Unbound* (a) Jacobean 2. *A Game at Chesse* (b) Restoration 3. *The Country Wife* (c) Augustan 4. *The Vanity of Human Wishes* (d) Romantic

889. James Boswell, the biographer of Samuel Johnson, was a distinguished author on his own. Identify his books from the following:
(a) *An Account of Barcelona* (b) *The Venetian Journal* (c) *London Journal* (d) *Boswell in Amsterdam*

890. Match the authors with their books.
1. *Rural Rides* (a) Axel Munthe 2. *The Last of Mohicans* (b) William Corbett 3. *The Story of San Michele* (c) Joseph Conrad 4. *Nostromo* (d) James Fennimore Cooper

891. *A Modest Proposal* (1729), a sarcastic and bitter pamphlet by Swift, proposed
(a) the killing of all female children at birth (b) the imposition of a tax on the families of lunatics (c) the imposition of a tax on beggars'

incomes (d) The bringing up of babies as prime
meat for sale

892. In which book do the two characters Tweedledum
and Tweedledee appear?
(a)*Alice's Adventures in Wonderland* (b) *Through the
Looking-glass* (c) *The Hunting of the Snark* (d) *Sylvie
and Bruno*

893. Who first expounded the doctrine of art for art's
sake?
(a) Max Beerbohm (b) Oscar Wilde (c) Theophile
Gautier (d) Stephane Mallarme

894. One of the most important English literary critics
of all time, he wrote *Culture and Anarchy* and
Essays in Criticism (First and Second Series). T.S.
Eliot, F.R. Leavis and Raymond Williams have
been influenced by him. Who is he?
(a) Dr. Johnson (b) William Hazlitt (c) Matthew
Arnold (d) I.A. Richards

895. When their husband died issueless, the mother-
in-law of two widowed queens ordered them to
get impregnated by a smelly and savage-looking
hermit. This started happenings of epic
dimensions. Which epic?
(a)*The Mahabharata* (b) *Nibelungenlied* (c) *Iliad*
(c) *Volsunga Saga*

896. This American humorist came to fame with the

publication of *My Life and Hard Times,* although this was not his first book. Who is he?

(a) James Thurber (b) Mark Twain (c) Stephen Leacock (d) Ogden Nash

897. *Walden* is considered a very important book in the history of American thought and literature. Who wrote it?

(a) Edwin Arlington Robinson (b) Walt Whitman (c) Henry David Thoreau (d) James Russell Lowell

898. The name Roderick seems to have caught the fancy of poets and novelists, for there are at least four of them in titles of novels and poems. Match the titles with the authors.

1. *Roderick, Vision of Don* (poem) (a) Southey 2. *Roderick Hudson* (novel) (b) Smollett 3. *Roderick Random* (novel) (c) Walter Scott 4. *Roderick, the Last of the Goths* (poem) (d) Henry James

899. Who was the author of *Self-help,* the book which preaches industry, thrift, and self-improvement as cardinal virtues?

(a) William Wain (b) Tom Paine (c) Samuel Smiles (d) Josiah Wedgwood

11

FOR THINE IS THE KINGDOM

900. What is the total number of books in the Bible, Old and New Testaments taken together?
(a) 59 (b) 66 (c) 49 (d) 71

901. What is the total number of books in the Old Testament?
(a) 39 (b) 26 (c) 47 (d) 19

902. Which is the earliest book of the New Testament?
(a) Matthew (b) Mark (c) Luke (d) John

903. In *A Portrait of the Artist as a Young Man* Stephen Dedaluas reflects: '*March 21, night.* Free. Soul free and fancy free. Let the dead bury the dead. And let the dead marry the dead.'
The reference to burying is Biblical. In which Books of the Bible do you find the sentence, in a slightly different form?
(a) I Samuel (b) Matthew (c) Luke (d) Job

904.   'Jack, eating rotten cheese, did say,
          Like Samson, I my thousands slay;

I vow, quoth Roger, so you do.
And with the self-same weapon too'.
This is attributed to Benjamin Franklin, and the allusion is biblical. Which book of the Bible do you turn to for an explanation?
(a) Daniel (b) Judges (c) II Chronicles (d) Genesis

905. Identify the Book of the New Testament which has: 'What shall it profit a man, if he shall gain the whole world, and lose his soul'?
(a) Matthew (b) Mark (c) Luke (d) John

906. Tell which of the following Books belong to the Old Testament.
(a) I Kings (b) Psalms (c) Ecclesiastes (d) Revelation

907. The name of Dietrich Bonhoeffer (1906-45) is remembered with affection and reverence for his courageous stand
(a) in opposing Stalin's suppression of the churches and the purge of intellectuals. Arrested and liquidated (b) in opposing the Nazis, who arrested him, put him in the concentration camp, and executed him (c) in supporting Margaret Sanger's birth control movement when the entire church was opposed to it (d) in campaigning for a Jewish homeland in Palestine much against the wishes of the government, which put him in prison

908. One of the following isn't apocryphal (see 938).
Which?
(a) Habakkuk   (b)   Esdras   (c)   Tobit
(d) Ecclesiasticus

909. Tell which of the books belong to the New
Testament?
(a) Ephesians (b) Jeremiah (c) The Song of
Solomon (d) Jude

910. When did the Authorized or King James version
of the Bible in English appear?
(a)   1598 (b) 1605 (c) 1611 (d) 1623

911. What is the total number of Books in the New
Testament?
(a)   29 (b) 27 (c) 31 (d) 6

912. As you sow, so you reap—this is originally a
Biblical phrase, adapted, 'Whatsoever a man
soweth, that shall he also reap' being the text.
Which Book does it belong to?
(a) Galatians (b) Ephesians (c) Proverbs
(d) Lamentations

913. 'The reward of sin is death: that's hard.' Faustus in
his study, considering the various studies
available to him, comments about theology. He
has quoted Jerome's Bible. What is it?
(a) A fourteenth century English Bible prepared
by St. Jerome (b) A Hebraic edition, revised and

corrected by St. Jerome (c) A Latin translation, known as the Vulgate (d) A parallel Greek and Latin text compiled by Jerome

914. ' "What is truth", said jesting Pilate; and would not stay for an answer'—Thus begins Bacon's essay 'Of Truth'. Which Book of the Bible reports Pilate's jest?
(a)Matthew (b) Mark (c) Luke (d) John

915. Which book of the Old Testament has the following verse? 'Vanity of vanities, saith the Preacher, vanity of vanities; all is vanity.'
(a) Proverbs (b) Job (c) Ecclesiastes (d) Isaiah

916. 'Rise up, my love, my fair one, and come away. For, lo, the winter is past, the rain is over and gone.The flowers appear on the earth; the time of singing of the birds is come, and the voice of the turtle is heard in our land.' Identify the Book in which this is to be found.
(a) Psalms (b) Proverbs (c) Song of Solomon (d) Ezekiel

917. 'It is easier for a cannibal to enter the Kingdom of Heaven through the eye of a rich man's needle than it is for any other foreigner to read the terrible German script.'— Mark Twain was referring to the Gothic script; however he twisted the original Biblical sentence about the camel and the rich man. Which Book of the Bible has the sentence?

(a) Ruth (b) Matthew (c) Genesis (d) Isaiah

918. The Prodigal son goes to a far country and wastes his substance with riotous living; then, during a mighty famine he has to fill his belly with 'the husks that swine did eat'. Naturally he returns home, and his father— welcomes him with new clothes and fatted calf.
Which Book of the Bible tells the story?
(a) Genesis (b) John (c) Titus (d) Luke

919. In 'The Lost Leader' Browning attacks Wordsworth for deserting the liberal cause, the poem beginning, 'Just for a handful of silver he left us...' The reference, of course, is to Judas and the thirty pieces of silver for which he betrayed Jesus. Which Book of the New Testament tells the story?
(a) Matthew (b) Mark (c) Luke (d) John

920. *The Seven Pillars of Wisdom* by Lawrence of Arabia takes its title from the Bible. From where precisely?
(a) Deuteronomy (b) Exodus (c) Proverbs (d) Ecclesiastes

921. The expression 'God save the king' is biblical and occurs in
(a) I Samuel (b) II Samuel (c) II Kings (d) II Chronicles

922. Chaucer's Wife of Bath is full of praise for King Solomon, 'the wise kyng, daun Solomon' who had wives more than one. How many women did

Solomon have?
(a) 16 wives and 78 concubines (b) 237 wives and 193 concubines (c) 900 wives (d) 700 wives and 300 concubines

923. In which Book of the New Testament do you find this? 'In my Father's house are many mansions.'
(a) Matthew (b) Mark (c) Luke (d) John

924. Many would agree that 'much study is a weariness of flesh', and a large number of teachers, therefore, stop reading after their M.A. or Ph.D. Which Book of the Bible are they paying their homage to?
(a) Esther (b) The Acts (c) Ecclesiastes (d) Revelation

925. Identify the Book of the New Testament which has this: 'Resist not evil: but whosoever shall smite thee on thy right cheek, turn to him the other also.'
(a) Matthew (b) Mark (c) Luke (d) John

926. 'For dust thou art, and unto dust shalt thou return.' Which Book of the Old Testament has it?
(a) Genesis (b) Exodus (c) Job (d) Leviticus

927. 'Thrice welcome, thrice blessed'—the 'thrice' is used because
(a) it is an auspicious number (b) it is the Hebrew superlative (c) it is the number of the Holy Trinity (d) it is the number most often used in the New

Testament

928. What's wrong with a fly in the ointment? The Bible tells you what: 'Dead flies cause the ointment of the apothecary to send forth a stinking savour...' In which book does it do so?
(a) Proverbs (b) Numbers (c) Judges (d) Ecclesiastes

929. Millions of children have been flogged by their parents or schools on the maxim, 'Spare the rod and spoil the child'. They have the Bible to thank for. Which Book says, 'He that spareth his rod hateth his son: but he that loveth him chasteneth him betimes'?
(a) I Corinthians (b) I Samuel (c) Proverbs (d) Ecclesiastes

930. The title of Andre Gide's novel *Strait Is the Gate* (strait meaning narrow) is straight from the Bible. Which Book of the Bible?
(a) Matthew (b) Mark (c) Luke (d) John

931. Exodus mentions ten plagues. Which of the following are on its list?
(a) Frogs (b) Lice (c) Cockroaches (d) Flies

932. 'The Wicked Bible' of 1631 is so called because it dropped a 'not' from one of the prohibitions of the Ten Commandments. Which is it?
(a) not commit adultery (b) not covet the

neighbour's house or wife (c) not kill (d) not bear false witness

933. Of the Book of Job an intellectual lady, also a novelist, wrote: 'I read the Book of Job last night—I don't think God comes well out of it'. Who could it be?
(a) Katherine Mansfield (b) Virginia Woolf (c) Mary McCarthy (d) Erica Jong

934. One particular Bible is to be found most frequently in American hotel rooms. Which is it?
(a) The Gutenberg Bible (b) The Gideon Bible (c) The Mazarin Bible (d) The Authorized Version, 1611

935. Shaw's play, *Back to Methuselah*, refers to the grandfather of Noah, who lived exceptionaly long. How long?
(a) 140 Years (b) 210 Years (c) 569 Years (d) 969 Years

936. To express her sorrow, Emily Dickinson called herself. 'Empress of Calvary'. Where does the world Calvary, a translation of the Aramaic *gulgutha*, occur?
(a) Matthew (b) Mark (c) Luke (d) John

937. In *The Waste Land*, T.S. Eliot writes:
'By the waters of Leman I sat down and wept...
There is an echo of the Bible: 'By the rivers of

Babylon, there we sat down, yea, we wept, when we remembered Zion'. Which Book?

(a) Psalms (b) Exodus (c) Ruth (d) Isaiah

938. The Apocrypha (from which apocryphal, meaning not authentic) are those books included in the Greek Septuagint and the Latin Vulgate versions not counted as genuine by the Jews. Which Christian denomination declared them inauthentic?

(a) Roman Catholics (b) Protestants (c) The Orthodox Eastern Church (d) Lutherans

939. The New English Bible is not recognized by one of the churches. Which?

(a) Roman Catholic (b) Church of England (c) Lutheran (d) Baptist

940. In 1961 a modern English translation of the New Testament was published. This was followed by a translation of the Old Testament and Apocrypha in 1970. What are these translations together called?

(a) The Revised Standard Version (b) The New Authorized Version (c) A New Translation of the New and Old Testaments (d) The New English Bible

941. Which is the first complete translation of the Bible into English?

(a) William Tyndale's (b) Miles Coverdale's

(c) By Wyclif and his followers (d) The 'Authorized Version' of 1611

942. Which is the earliest Old Testament text?
(a) The Hebrew text Codex Babylonicus Petropolitanus (b) The Samaritan text of the Pentateuch (the first five books of the Old Testament) (c) The Greek version known as the Septuagint (d) Jerome's Latin text, known as the Vulgate

943. When were the four Gospels written?
(a) A.D. 212-238 (b) A.D. 300-400 (c) A.D. 65-90 (d) A.D 10-35

944. Which is the shortest of the Gospels?
(a) Matthew (b) Mark (c) Luke (d) John

945. Which Book of the Old Testament has this verse?
'Whither thou goest, I will go, and where thou lodgest, I will lodge: thy people shall be my people, and thy God my God.'
(a) Exodus (b) Esther (c) Psalms (d) Ruth

946. 'Physician, heal thyself.' Identify the source.
(a) Matthew (b) Mark (c) Luke (d) John

947. What was the punishment of the woman taken in adultery in John 8: 3-11?
(a) She was ordered to be stoned to death (b) She was ordered to marry the adulterer (c) She was

asked to sin no more (d) She was banished from her homeland

948. The Arthurian romances have, as their central theme, the quest for the Holy Grail. What was it? (a) Christ's shroud (b) An eternal flame given to Joseph of Arimathea by Jesus (c) The cross on which Jesus was crucified (d) Jesus's cup at the Last Supper in which Joseph of Arimathea caught some of Jesus's blood at Crucifixion

949. Where is the story of the Good Samaritan told ? (a) Job (b) Luke (c) Judges (d) John

12

WHODUNIT

950. In whose novel does Aunt Agatha strike terror into the heart of her nephew, quite the unheroic hero?
(a) John Wayne (b) F. Scott Fitzgerald (c) P.G. Wodehouse (d) James Thurber

951. *The Autobiography of a Supertramp* was written by W.H. Davies ('What is this life, if full of care'). Later another tramp's story, superbly told, *Down and Out in the Streets of Paris and London*, was written by an author some of whose books have been read by millions. Who is he?
(a) George Orwell (b) Henry Miller (c) Allen Ginsberg (d) Arthur Koestler

952. He had been called the father of Soviet literature and the founder of the doctrine of Socialist realism. A storywriter, novelist, and dramatist — who is he?
(a) Anton Chekhov (b) Nikolai Gogol (c) Maxim Gorky (d) Alexei Tolstoy

953. *Absalom, Absalom!, Intruder in the Dust, As I Lay Dying,* and *The Sound and the Fury* are some of the books of this Nobel Prize-winning (1949) American author. Who is he?
(a) Eugene O'Neill (b) Pearl S. Buck (c) William Faulkner (d) John Steinbeck

954. Which science fiction writer wrote *Pebbles in the Sky*?
(a) J.G. Ballard (b) Isaac Asimov (c) Ray Bradbury (d) Arthur C. Clarke

955. Who, among the following travel writers, wrote *The Great Railway Bazaar*?
(a) Eric Newby (b) Laurence Van der Post (c) Bruce Chatwin (d) Paul Theroux

956. *Small Is Beautiful* was written by
(a) E. Schumacher (b) Vance Packard (c) Ralph Nader (d) Bruno Bettelheim

957. Born in Germany, daughter of a Polish Jewish solicitor, she sought refuge in England in 1939. In 1951 she married an Indian architect and lived for 24 years in India. She wrote *Esmond in India* and *A New Dominion*, among other novels. Who is she?
(a) Rosamond Lehmann (b) Ruth Prawer Jhabvala (c) Ivory Shakespearewallah (d) Juliette Bannerjee

958. Georg Lukacs, Christopher Caudwell, Raymond Williams, and Terry Eagleton : what have they in common?
(a) All Marxist critics (b) All disciples of F.R. Leavis (c) All authors of the Left Book Club (d) All made their debut in *The New Statesman*

959. About one in the circle of Dr. Johnson, Garrick said. 'He wrote like an angel but talked like poor Poll', although Johnson himself wrote that he adorned whatever he touched. To give you a hint, he edited a journal called *The Bee*. Who was he?
(a) Richard Savage (b) The Earl of Chesterfield (c) Oliver Goldsmith (d) Edward Gibbon

960. A husband-and-wife team, Peter and Iona Opie researched together on children and produced such important books as *The Lore and Language of School Children* and *Children's Games in Street and Playground*. What is considered to be their major work?
(a) *Fairy Tales of Ancient Britain* (b) *Baby Talk* (c) *Lullabies for Little Ones* (d) *Oxford Dictionary of Nursery Rhymes*

961. The story of terror, *Frankenstein*, was written by
(a) Bram Stoker (b) Monk Lewis (c) Mrs. Radcliffe (d) Mary Shelley

962. Who wrote *King Solomon's Mines*?
(a) R.M. Ballantyne (b) R.L. Stevenson (c) Wilkie

Collins (d) Rider Haggard

963. Charles Lutwidge Dodgson was a lecturer in mathematics at Christ Church College in Oxford. What did he write that made him famous?
(a) *Winnie the Pooh* (b) *Alice's Adventures in Wonderland* (c) *The Tale of Peter Rabbit* (d) *Wind in the Willows*

964. Who is the detective story writer, once himself a Pinkerton detective, who wrote *The Maltese Falcon*?
(a) Raymond Chandler (b) Dashiell Hammett (c) Nicholas Freeling (d) Ed McBain

965. *Peter Rabbit,* a children's classic, was written by
(a) Enid Blyton (b) A.A. Milne (c) Beatrix Potter (d) Arthur Ransome

966. *The Story of Art* is one of the most popular books on art, widely used as a textbook in many places. Who wrote it?
(a) Herbert Read (b) G.M. Trevelyan (c) Arnold Toynbee (d) Ernst Gombrich

967. Who wrote the film version of Shaw's *Pygmalion, My Fair Lady*?
(a) Bernard Shaw (b) Jerome Kern (c) Guy Bolton (d) Alan Jay Lerner

968. The most popular of his plays is *The Inspector*

General. Who is he?
(a) Nikolai Gogol (b) Anton Chekhov
(c) Alexander Pushkin (d) Leo Tolstoy

969. Whose lawyer-detective is Perry Mason?
(a) Ellery Queen's (b) Dick Francis's (c) Erle Stanley Gardner's (d) Margery Allingham's

970. A distinguished writer on cricket and a popular detective story writer, this man wrote *Filmi Filmi Inspector Ghote*, on criminal goings on in the Bombay film world. Who is he?
(a) Michael Gilbert (b) Ellis Peters (c) H.R.F. Keating (d) P.D. James

971. His experience as a professional champion steeplechase jockey made him a specialist in racing crime fiction. Who is he?
(a) Michael Innes (b) Ngaio Marsh (c) H.R.F. Keating (d) Dick Francis

972. *The Wind in the Willows* has been a children's classic since 1908, and even today new editions, with new illustrations, keep coming out. Who wrote it?
(a) Robert Louis Stevenson (b) A.A. Milne (c) Kenneth Gahame (d) Enid Blyton

973. Marquis de Sade, who lent his name to sadism—infliction of pain on others to derive sexual pleasure—wrote a number of books considered

211

by some to be obscene. Which is his most famous book?
(a) *Roxana* (b) *Clea* (c) *Justine* (d) *Phaedra*

974. In *Last Year in Marienbad*, Alain Resnais, the French filmmaker, used the screenplay of a novelist considered to be the originator of the French New Novel. Who is the screenplay by?
(a) Alain Robe-Grillet (b) Jean Cocteau
(c) Marguerite Duras (d) Francoise Sagan

975. Jacob Grimm, one of the brothers of Grimms' Fairy Tales, was also eminent in another field, in which his scholarship is highly regarded even today. Which field is it?
(a) History (b) Music (c) Philology (d) Philosophy

976. The story of transposed heads, dramatized by Girish Karnad in *Hayavadana*, originally comes from *Kathasaritsagara*, although Karnad went to another author for the retold story. Who is that author?
(a) Thomas Mann (b) Friedrich Durrenmatt
(c) Jean Genet (d) August Strindberg

977. Here are four works of different genres which use 'golden' as part of the title of their books. Relate them with the authors.
1. *The Golden Notebook* (a) Sir James Frazer 2. *The Golden Ass* (b) Doris Lessing 3. *The Golden Bough* (c) Apeleius 4. *The Golden Bowl* (d) Henry James

978. *Zen and the Art of Motorcycle Maintenance* was written by
(a) Irving Howe (b) R.M. Pirsig (c) R. Terkel (d) R. Kluger

979. Who wrote The *Castle of Otranto*, the Gothic novel?
(a) Mrs. Radcliffe (b) Monk Lewis (c) Horace Walpole (d) Thomas Love Peacock

980. In 1984 an important novel—really a superb biography—appeared in England on the American Civil War and Abraham Lincoln. Who is the author of *Lincoln*?
(a) Gore Vidal (b) Philip Roth (c) Saul Bellow (d) Terence Armstrong

981. Who wrote *Future Shock*?
(a) E. Schumacher (b) Vance Packard (c) Alvin Toffler (d) B.F. Skinner

982. *The Second Sex* was written by
(a) Simone de Beauvoir (b) Germaine Greer (c) Erica Jong (d) Konrad Lorenz

983. *Trent's Last Case* (1913) has been called the prototype of the detective novel. Who wrote it?
(a) Hilaire Belloc (b) Agatha Christie (c) G.K. Chesterton (d) E.C. Bentley

984. *A Portrait of the Artist as a Young Man* was written

by James Joyce. Who wrote *Portrait of the Artist as a Young Dog?*
(a) Samuel Beckett (b) Sean O'Faolin (c) J.P. Donleavy (d) Dylan Thomas

985. *The Well of Loneliness* is perhaps the earliest novel (1928) depicting lesbianism. Who wrote it?
(a) Nancy Mitford (b) Virginia Woolf (c) Germaine Greer (d) Radclyffe Hall

986. A Greek poet, he was awarded the 1979 Nobel Prize in literature. The English translation of his poems is to be found in the selection *The Sovereign Sun*. Who is he?
(a) George Seferis (b) Odysseus Elytis (c) Constantine Cavafy (d) Aristotle Socrates Onassis

987. *The True-born Englishman, The Shortest Way with Dissenters, Life and Adventures of Mrs. Duncan Campbell,* and *Roxana* are some of his works, although his most famous book has not been mentioned here. Identify the author.
(a) Defoe (b) Nash (c) Deloney (d) Fielding

988. Who wrote *The Compleat Angler?*
(a) Roger Ascham (b) Izaak Walton (c) Thomas Brown (d) Robert Burton

989. Who wrote *The Enemies of Promise?*
(a) Chistopher Caudwell (b) Lord David Cecil

(c) Albert Camus (d) Cyril Connolly

990. *Studies in a Dying Culture* (1938), is a seminal work on the Marxist theory of art. Who is the author? (a) Friedrich Engels (b) Eric Fromm (c) Georg Lukacs (d) Christopher Caudwell

991. One of the earliest tracts against press censorship, *Areopagitica*, was written by (a) Sir Henry Wotton (b) Sir Philip Sidney (c) John Milton (d) Jonathan Swift

992. The author of *The Thief's Journal* has actually been a thief. Who is he? (a) Albert Camus (b) Jean Giradoux (c) Paul Eluard (d) Jean Genet

993. This granddaughter of Charles Darwin wrote a delightful autobiographical account of Cambridge in *Period Piece*. Who is she? (a) Muriel Spark (b) Q.D. Leavis (c) Gwen Raverat (d) Mary Mitford

994. Who was the author of *Silent Spring*, one of the earlier books on environmental pollution? (a) Vance Packard (b) Linus Pauling (c) Rachel Carson (d) Gunnar Myrdal

995. *I, Claudius* and *Claudius the God* are remarkable historical novels about the Romans. The author also wrote *Wife to Mr Milton*, again a historical

novel. Who is the author?
(a) C.V. Wedgwood (b) Christopher Hill
(c) Robert Graves (d) Alberto Moravia

996. *Slowly Down the Ganges* is a memorable account of
a boat journey on the Ganga. Who is the author?
(a) Eric Newby (b) Paul Theroux (c) James
Cameron (d) Geoffrey Moorhouse

997. He wrote *Nexus, Sexus,* and *Plexus,* but two of his
more notorious books are still banned in India.
Who is the author?
(a) John Cleland (b) Henry Miller (c) James Joyce
(d) Jack Kerouac

998. Who wrote *Gentlemen Prefer Blondes*?
(a) Penelope Mortimer (b) Anita Loos (c) Fanny
Hill (d) Muriel Spark

999. In an important modern novel the hero, a jewish
intellectual, writes unsent letters about himself
and civilization to the living and the dead. Which
is it?
(a) Isaac Bashevis Singer's *A Friend of Kafka*
(b) Bernard Malamud's *A New Life* (c) Philip
Roth's *The Ghost Writer* (d) Saul Bellow's *Herzog*

1000. The characters Monica Douglas (famous mostly
for mathematics), Rose Stanley (famous for sex),
Eunice Gardiner (spritely gymnastics and
glamorous swimming), Mary Macgregor (famed

as a silent lump), are all characters in a novel about a teacher at the Maria Blaines School for Girls. Which novel is it?

(a) *Farewell, My Pets* (b) *Golden Day* (c) *The Prime of Miss Jean Brodie* (d) *Past Perfect*

BAKER'S DOZEN

In spite of the vigilance of the author, editor, and proof-reader, a few questions may have been repeated. In order to make up for this, we are doing what bakers used to do to avoid being punished for supplying short, viz., we are throwing in some additional questions to make up for any shortage.

1a.   Pair the books by the same authors.
      1. *The Horse's Mouth* (a) *Jake's Thing* 2. *One Fat Englishman* (b) *Herself Surprised* 3. *To Be a Pilgrim* (c)*Ultramarine* 4. *Under the Volcano* (d) *Mister Johnson*

2a.   The Abbey Theatre, Dublin, became famous at the beginning of the twentieth century because it put up one of the following plays:
      (a) First English performance of *Doll's House* (b) George Bernard Shaw's *Pygmalion* (c) Samuel Beckett's *Waiting for Godot* (d) J.M. Synge's *The Playboy of the Western World*

3a.   One of the following is not the work of Jean Anouilh. Which?
      (a) *Ring Round the Moon* (b) *Anitgone* (c) *Happy Days* (d) *Becket, or the Honour of God*

4a. Which among the following are the works of Samuel Beckett?
(a) *Endgame* (b) *Molloy* (c) *Come and Go* (d) *Breath*

5a. Of the following plays which one is by the Irish dramatist Brendan Behan?
(a) *The Quare Fellow* (b) *The Shadow of a Gunman*
(c) *Cock-a-Doodle Dandy* (d) *The Tinker's Wedding*

6a. Of the following one is by the Irish dramatist Sean O' Casey. Which ?
(a) *The Shadow of the Glen* (b) *The Tinker's Wedding*
(c) *The Rising of the Moon* (d) *Juno and the Paycock*

7a. Christopher Fry (b. 1907) is one of the successful verse dramatists of his age, sometimes compared with T.S. Eliot. Identify his play from the following.
(a) *A Phoenix Too Frequent* (b) *Mourning Becomes Electra* (c) *The Roman Spring of Mrs. Stone* (d) *Under Milk Wood*

8a. Of the following plays which was not written by Pirandello?
(a) *Six Characters in Search of an Author*
(b) *Rhinoceros* (c) *Henry IV* (d) *The Rules of the Game*

9a. Which among the following is not a play written jointly by W.H. Auden and Christopher Isherwood?
(a) *The Dog Beneath the Skin* (b) *The Ascent of F 6*

(c) *On the Frontier* (d) *The Age of Anxiety*

10a.   'Cecil B. de Mille,
        Rather against his will,
        Was persuaded to leave Moses
        Out of 'The War of Roses'.
        Know who wrote this?
        (a) Anon (b) Hilaire Belloc (c) Nicolas Bentley
        (d) E.Walsh

11a.   Nick Carraway and Daisy Buchanan are two
        characters in this famous novel which
        represented an era in American life. Identify the
        novel.
        (a) *Catcher in the Rye* (b) *A Diamond As Big As Ritz*
        (c) *Torrents of Spring* (d) *The Great Gatsby*

12a.   Whose creations are archie the cockroach and
        mehitabel the cat?
        (a) T.S. Eliot (b) Edward Lear (c) Don Marquis
        (d) Lewis Carroll

13a.   The number seven has featured as the title of
        many books. Of the following titles which one is
        bogus?
        (a) *Seven Lamps of Architecture* (b) *Seven Pillars of Wisdom* (c) *Seven Heavens of Delight* (d) *Seven Types of Ambiguity*

14a.   Match the authors' names with their pen names.
        1. Ricardo Reyes (a) J.H. Ross 2. Erle Stanley

Gardner (b) John Le Carre 3. T.E. Lawrence
(c) Pablo Neruda 4. David Cornwall (d) A.A. Fair

15a. Which recent Nobel Prize winner wrote the
following plays?: *A Dance of the Forests*, *The
Invention*, and *Death of the King's Horsemen?*
(a) Chinua Achebe (b) Buchi Emecheta (c) Wole
Soyinka (d) J.M. Coetzee

16a. 'But keep the wolf far thence, that's foe to men,
For with his nails he'll dig them up again'.
—Which poem or play, and who is the author?
(a) Shakespeare: *Measure for Measure* (b) T.S. Eliot:
Waste Land (c) John Webster: *The White Devil*
(d) John Marston: *The Malcontent*

17a. Match the authors with their books
1. Bhavabhuti (a) *Mrichchakatika* 2. Somadeva
(b) *Buddhacharita* 3. Asvaghosha (c) *Malatimadhava*
4. Sudraka (d) *Kathasaritsagara*

18a. '…This grew; I gave commands;
Then all smiles stopped together.'
Who wrote this?
(a) Rupert Brooke (b) Peter Sellers (c) Robert
Browning (d) Spike Milligan

19a. In which story/play/poem does the character of
Willy Loman appear?
(a) Graham Greene: *The Quiet American*
(b) William Faulkner: *The Rievers* (c) Tennessee

Williams : *The Glass Menagerie* (d) Arthur Miller: *Death of a Salesman*

20a. 'And a woman is only a woman, but a good cigar is a smoke'. Identify the MCP who said this .
(a) Rudyard Kipling (b) Winston Churchill (c) Bishop Blougram (d) Dean Inge

21a. A Canadian economist and humorist, he has written a memorable essay on opening an account in a bank. Apart from standard works on economics, he is the author of *Literary Lapses.* Who is he?
(a) Edward Lear (b) Richard Leavey (c) Charles Lawrence (d) Stephen Leacock

22a. Many people think that the best book on Calcutta is *Calcutta,* by
(a) James Cameron (b) Dominique Lapierre (c) Clive James (d) Geoffrey Moorhouse

23a. Who wrote *The Vanity of Human Wishes?*
(a) Jonathan Swift (b) Alexander Pope (c) Dr. Johnson (d) Thomas Gray

24a. Who was Countee Cullen?
(a) Black American poet (b) Popular writer of burlesques (c) Famous Broadway dramatist (d) Hollywood scriptwriter

ANSWERS

1. (a); 2 (a); 3 (c); 4 (b); 5 (d); 6 (c); 7 (c); 8 (a); 9 (a); 10 (d); 11 (b); 12 (b); 13 (a); 14 (a); 15 (c); 16 (c); 17 (b); 18 (c); 19 (c); 20 (b); 21 (a) ; 22 (d); 23 (b); 24 (c); 25 (c); 26 (d); 27 (d); 28 (c); 29 (d); 30 (a); 31 (d); 32 (a); 33 (a); 34 (b); 35 (c); 36 (a); 37 (b); 38 (c); 39 (b); 40 (a); 41 (c); 42 (b); 43 (c); 44 (c); 45 (a); 46 (c); 47 (b); 48 (c); 49 (c); 50 (c); 51(b); 52 (a); 53 (a); 54 (d); 55 (d); 56 (b); 57 (a); 58 (d); 59 (a); 60 (b); 61 (b); 62 (d); 63 (c); 64 (b); 65 (c); 66 (d) in *Zuleika Dobson*; 67 (c); 68 (b); 69 (b); 70 (c); 71 (c); 72 (b) ; 73 (d); 74 (c); against Ruskin; 75 (a); 76 (a); 77 (a), Elizabeth Arden; 78 (c); 79 (b); 80 (c); 81: 1b, 2d, 3a, 4c; 82 (a); 83 (c); 84 (b); 85 (d); 86 (c); 87 (b); 88 (b); 89 (b); 90 (c); 91 (b); 92 (c); 93 (d); 94 (c); 95 (c); 96 (d); 97 (a), (c); 98 (d); Oscar Fingal O'Flahertie Wills; 99 (d); 100 (a); 101 (a); 102 (d); 103 (c); 104 (d); 105 (d); 106 (d), in 1954; 107 none; 108 (d); 109 (d); 110 all; 111 (d); 112 (b); 113 (c); 114 (b); 115 (d); 116 (c); 117 (b); 118 (a); 119 (c) by Sean O'Casey; 120 (d), her grandfather taught Dr. Johnson; 121 (d) 122: 1c, 2a, 3b, 4d; 123 (a); 124 (a); 125 (a) in *Eclogues;* 126 (c); 127 (d); 128 (a); 129 (c); 130: 1b, 2c, 3a, 4d; 131: 1d, 2c, 3b, 4a; 132: 1d, 2a, 3b, 4c; 133 (c); 134 b, Gutenberg; 135 (c); 136 (d); 137 (a), more than 1507 million; 138 (d); 139 (b), more than 315, 000, 000 copies a year; 140 (c) queueing; 141 (d), Grove Press edition of *Fanny Hill,* in Germany, England, and Japan; 142 (c); 143 (a); 144 (b); 145 (c); 146 (c) 147 (a);

148 (a); 149 (c); 150 (a); 151 (d), Caxton, *The Dictes or Sayingis of the Philosophres* ; 152 (c); 153 (d); 154 (d); 155 (a); 156 (d); 157 (d); 158 (c); 159 (a); 160 (a), Regina Vs. Penguin Books, Penguin acquitted; 161 (c); 162 (a), 1731; 163 (b); 164 (a) , (b), and (c); 165 (c); 166 (b); 167 (d), *Uncle Tom's Cabin* 1852; 168 (c), 1885-1972; 169 (c); 170 (a), Willaim Golding; 171 (b); 172 (a); 173 (c); 174 (d); 175 1c, 2a, 3b, 4d; 176 (a), (d); 177 (a); 178 (d); 179 (c); 180 (a); 181 (a); 182 (b); 183 (c) ; 184 (b); 185 (b); 186 (d); 187 (d); 188 (a); 189 (c); 190 (c); 191 (d), Mark Twain said that; 192 (a); 193 (c); 194 (a); 195 (b), Arthur Hallam; 196 (c); 197 (a), 4'6"; 198 Zelda; 199 (a); 200 (b); 201 (d); 202 (a), at the age of 18; 203 (c); 204 (c); 205 (b); 206 (c); 207 (a); 208 (a); 209 (b); 210 (a); 211 (c); 212 (a); 213 (d), Fellow, Christ Church College, Oxford; 214 (a); 215 (b); 216 (b); 217 (b); 218 (b); 219 (d); 220 all; 221 (b); 222 1c, 2d, 3a, 4b; 223 (a); 224 (c); 225 (a); 226 (a); 227 (a); 228 (c); 229 (b); 230 (c); 231 (b), 1924; 232 (d); 233 (b); 234 (a); 235 (b); 236 (d); 237 (c); 238 (d); 239 (a); 240 (b); 241 (d); 242 (b); 243 (d); 244 (c); 245 (b); 246 (b), 1960, *The Guide* ; 247 (b); 248 (c); 249 (a); 250 (c); 251 (b), (d); 252 (a), (c), (d); 253 (b); 254 (d); 255 (b); 256 (b); 257 (d); 258 (d); 259 (a); 260 (c); 261 (c); 262 (a), (b), (c); 263 1c, 2d, 3a, 4b; 264 (c); 265 (c); 266 (a); 267 (d); 268 1c, 2d, 3a, 4b; 269 (a); 270 (c); 271 1c, 2d, 3a, 4b; 272 (c); 273 (c); 274 (b); 275 (b); 276 (c); 277 (b); 278 (c); 279 (d); 280 (b) Sahitya Akademi, (d) Bharatiya Jnanpith; 281 (b); 282 1b, 2c, 3a, 4d; 283 (c), *Waiting for the Mahatma* ; 284 (d); 285 (d); 286 (d); 287 (c); 288 (d); 289 (c); 290 (a), (d); 291 all except (b); 292 (c); 293 (a), *A Passage to England* ; 294 (b); 295 (c); 296 (a); 297 (c); 298 (d); 299 (d); 300 1b,2a,3d,4c; 301 (c); 302 (b);

303 (c); 304 (d); 305 (c); 306 1c,2a,3d,4b; 307 (c);
308 (a),(b);309 (c); 310 (b); 311 (c); 312 (b); 313 (b); 314 (c);
315 (a); 316 (c); 317 (d), by U.R. Anantha Murthy,
translated by A.K. Ramanujan; 318 (a); 319 (b),(c), (d);
320 (d); 321 (d); 322 (c); 323 (c); 324 (a),*Crossing of
Rivers* ; 325 (b), the exclamation mark is missing; 326 (c);
327 (a); 328 (b); 329 (c); 330 (d); 331 (d); 332 (b); 333 (a),
(d); 334 (d); 335 (a); 336 (c); 337 (b); 338 (c); 339 (a), by
Sashi Tharoor; 340 (a); 341 (c); 342 (b); 343 (b); 344 (d); 345
(c); 346 (b); 347 (d), the rest are by Sophocles; 348 1b, 2c,
3d, 4a; 349 1c, 2a, 3d, 4b; 350 1c, 2b, 3a, 4d; 351 (b), by
Ovid; 352 all; 353 (b); 354 (b); 355 (d); 356 (b); 357 (b);
358 (b); 359 (c); 360 (a); 361 (c); 362 (a), (b), (c); 363 (a);
364 (c); 365 (c); 366 (c); 367 1c, 2d, 3a, 4b; 368 (b); 369 (d);
370 (a); 371 (a); 372 (d); 373 (b), the rest are by Euripides;
374 (b); 375 (c); 376 (d); 377 (d); 378 (a),(b); 379 (d);
380 (c); 381 (d); 382 (c); 383 (b); 384 (a); 385 (b); 386 (c);
387 (c); 388 (d); 389 (b); 390 (a); 391 (c); 392 (d); 393 (a);
394 (c); 395 (c); 396 (b); 397 (b); 398 (a); 399 (b); 400 (d);
401 (a); 402 (c); 403(d), largest number acquired by the
Folger Shakespeare Library, Washington, D.C., about
80; 404 (a); 405 (b); 406 (a); 407 (d); 408 (d); 409 (a); 410 (c),
Portia's assumed name as a lawyer; 411 (d), 'I would
give you some violets, but they withered all when my
father died'; 412 (b); 413 (b); 414 1b, 2a, 3d, 4c; 415 (a);
416 (c); 417 (c); 418 (b); 419 (d); 420 (d), Falstaff; 421 (c);
422 1a, 2d, 3b, 4c; 423 (d); 424 (a); 425 (b); 426 (a), in
Travesties; 427 (a), *The Rehearsal*; 428 (c); 429 (b); 430 (c),
(d); 431 (a); 432 (c); 433 (b); 434 (c); 435 (a), (c), (d); 436 (b);
437 (a), *Le Bourgeois Gentilhomme*; 438 (a), (b), (c);
439 1d, 2c, 3a, 4b; 440 (a), (b), (d); 441 (b); 442 (b); 443 (d);

444 (c); 445 (b); 446 (c); 447 (c); 448 (c), by Marlowe;
449 (d); 450 (c); 451 (c); 452 (a); 453 (c); 454 (a); 455 (c);
456 (b), (c); 457 (d); 458 (a); 459 (a); 460 (c), a Hollywood
script writer; 461, all are quite short, (b) is 30 seconds
long, with neither actors, nor dialogue; 462 (c); 463 (c);
464 (c); 465 (a) and (b) are by Racine, the other two by
Corneille; 466 (a); 467 (c); 468 (c); 469 (a); 470 (c); 471 (d);
472 (c); 473 (b); 474 (b); 475 (b); 476 (d); 477 (d); 478 (c);
479 (a); 480 (c), *A Ghost Sonata*; 481 (c); 482 (a); 483 (d), by
Strindberg; 484 (a), (b), (c); 485 (b); 486 (d); 487 (c);
488 (d); 489 (b); 490 (a) & (d) liked, (b) & (c) condemned;
491 (c); 492 (d); 493 (c); 494 (d); 495 (c); 496 (c); 497 (a);
498 (a); 499 (b),'Easter 1916'; 500 (c); 501 (d); 502 (d),
Sonnet 129; 503 (b); 504 (c); 505 (c); 506 (c); 507 (d), in
'Essay on Milton'; 508 (d); 509 (b); 510 (a); 511 (c); 512 (c);
513 (b); 514 (b); 515 (a); 516 (c); 517 (a), 'Elegy for Jane';
518 (d); 519 (b); 520 (b); 521 (d); 522 (a),'East Coker';
523 (a); 524 1d, 2a, 3b, 4c; 525 (b); 526 (d), in *The Marriage
of Heaven and Hell*; 527 (c); 528 (c); 529 (c); 530 (d);531 (c);
532 (c); 533 (a), (c), (d); 534 (b); 535 (d); 536 (c); 537 (c);
538 (b); 539 (c), *Bacchus and Ariadne*; 540 (c); 541 (c); 542
(b); 543 (d), in 'Fra Lippo Lippi'; 544 (a); 545 (a), 'Bagpipe
Music'; 546 (c); 547 (c), *English Bards and Scotch
Reviewers*; 548 (c), in *Poetics*; 549 (c), in 'In Memory of
W.B. Yeats'; 550 (a), in 'The Fisherman'; 551 (c); 552 (a);
553 (b); 554 (a), in Sonnet 94; 555 (d); 556 (d), in *Rubaiyat*
1.51; 557 (d); 558 (b); 559 (c); 560 (d); 561 (b); 562 (c), in
Atalanta in Calydon; 563 (a); 564 (c); 565 (c); 566 (c);
567 (c), 'Whispers of Immortality'; 568 (b), in 'West
Wind'; 569 (a); 570 (c); 571 (c); 572 (d); 573 (b); 574 (d);
575 (a); 576 (b), *Book of Songs*, 1827; 577 (c); 578 (c), 1557;

579 (a), (b), (d); 580 (b); 581 (a); 582 (b), (c), (d); 583 (a); 584 (a); 585 (b); 586 (d); 587 (c); 588 (c); 589 all; 590 (c); 591 (b); 592 (c); 593 (a), (c); 594 (c); 595 (b); 596 (b); 597 (d); 598 (c), e. g. 'Easter Wings'; 599 (c); 600 (b), (c), (d); 601 (d), *Ariel Poems* 1927-54; 602 (a), (b), (d); 603 (c); 604 (c); 605 (d); 606 (b); 607 (c); 608 (b); 609 (d); 610 (b); 611 (d); 612 (b); 613 (d); 614 (d); 615 (a); 616 (a), (b); 617 (c); 618 (c); 619 (d); 620 (a); 621 (c); 622 (c); 623 (a); 624(b); 625 (d); 626 (c); 627 (c); 628 (c), *She Stoops to Conquer*; 629 (d); 630 (d); 631 (b); 632 (a); 633 (c); 634 (c); 635 (b); 636 (b), in 'For the Fallen'; 637 (b); 638 (c); 639 (d); 640 (d); 641 (d); 642 (b); 643 (d); 644 (c), in 'Modern Fiction'; 645 (c); 646 (c); 647 (a); 648 (c); 649 (c), in *Tropic of Cancer*; 650 (d); 651 (a), 1640-89; 652 (c); 653 (c); 654 (d); 655 (c); 656 (d); 657 (d); 658 (c); 659 (d),(c), (a), (b); 660 1b, 2a, 3d, 4c; 661 1b, 2c, 3d, 4a; 662 (c), The filmed book is *Siddhartha*; 663 (d), *The Honourable Schoolboy; Tinker, Tailor, Soldier, Spy; and Smiley's People*; 664 1d, 2a, 3b, 4c; 665 (b); 666 (b); 667 (c); 668 (d); 669 (a); 670 (d); 671 (b); 672 (c); 673 (d); 674 (d); 675 (c); 676 (d); 677 (d); 678 (d); 679 (a), 1920; 680 (b); 681 (b); 682 (c); 683(c); 684 (b); 685 1b, 2c, 3d, 4a; 686 (b); 687 (c); 688 (d); 689 (d); 690 (c); 691 (d); 692 1c, 2d, 3a, 4b; 693 (c); 694 (b); 695 (d); 696 (b); 697 (d); 698 (c); 699 (d); 700 (c); 701 (c); 702 1d, 2c, 3b, 4a; 703 1a, 2b, 3d, 4f; 704 (c), (d); 705 (c); 706 (c); 707 (b); 708 (d), an anonymous collection; 709 (d); 710 (a); 711 (d); 712 (d); 713 (b); 714 (b); 715 (b); 716 (d); 717 (c), 1605 and 1616; 718 (c); 719 (d); 720 (a); 721 (c); 722 (a); 723 (d); 724 (c); 725 (d); 726 (b), (c); 727 (b); 728 (d); 729 (a), (c); 730 (a); 731 (d); 732 1c, 2d, 3b, 4a; 733 (c), *We'll to the Woods No More*, 1888; 734 (c); 735 (d); 736 (d), by

Kurt Vonnegut; 737 (b); 738 (a), by George Eliot; 739 (b); 740 (c); 741 (b); 742 (b); 743 (d); 744 (c); 745 (a); 746 (b), (c); 747 (b); 748 (d); 749 (a); 750 (c); 751 (a); 752 1c, 2d, 3a, 4b; 753 (d); 754 (a); 755 (c); 756 (c); 757 (b); 758 (c); 759 (b); 760 (a); 761 (c); 762 (a); 763 (c); 764 (c); 765 1d, 2b, 3a, 4c; 766 (d); 767 1c, 2d, 3b, 4a; 768 (b); 769 (b); 770 1c, 2d, 3a, 4b; 771 (d); 772 (c); 773 (c); 774 (b); 775 (a); 776 1c, 2a, 3b, 4d; 777 (c); 778 (c); 779 (d); 780 (b); 781 (c); 782 (c); 783 (c); 784 (c); 785 (a); 786 (c); 787 (d); 788 (c); 789 (c); 790 (c); 791 (b); 792 (b); 793 (d); 794 (b); 795 (c); 796 (d), Polish novelist, Nobel Prize 1905; 797 (c), by William Golding; 798 (c); 799 1c, 2d, 3a, 4b; 800 (a), (b), (d); 801 (b); 802 1d, 2c, 3a, 4b; 803 (d); 804 (d); 805 (d); 806 (b); 807 (c); 808 (d); 809 (c), (d); 810 1c, 2d, 3a, 4b; 811 (c); 812 1c, 2d, 3a, 4b; 813 (c), *The Tin Drum*; 814 (a); 815 (d); 816 (b); 817 (c); 818 (b), (c); 819 (c); 820 (d); 821 (c); 822 (b); 823 (a); 824 (d); 825 (c); 826 (c); 827 (b); 828 (c); 829 (d); 830 (d), (c), (a), (b); 831 1d, 2a, 3b, 4c; 832 1c, 2a, 3d, 4b; 833 (b), by Scott-Fitzgerald, while the others are by Salinger 834 (c); 835 (c); 836 (a); 837 (a); 838 (a), (d); 839 (a); 840 (c); 841 (a), (b), (d); 842 (a), (b), (d); 843 (b); 844 1d, 2c, 3a, 4b; 845 (a); 846 (b); 847 (b); 848 (d); 849 (a); 850 (b); 851 (d); by E.L. Doctorow; 852 (d); 853 (d); 854 (c); 855 (b); 856 (c) 857 (c), the third editor was T.S. Eliot; 858 (b); 859 (d); 860 (a); 861 (b); 862 1d, 2c, 3b, 4a; 863 (c); 864 (d); 865 (c); 866 (b); 867 1d, 2c, 3a, 4b; 868 (b); 869 (a); 870 (c); 871 (b); 872 1a, 2b, 3c, 4d; 873 1c, 2a, 3b, 4d; 874 (d), in *Culture and Anarchy*; 875 (b); 876 (c); 877 (b), nearly twenty years after Muhammad's death; 878 1d, 2c, 3b, 4a; 879 (c), Acts 9: 5, 6:14; 880 (b); 881 (b), (d); 882 (d); 883 (a), 1789 and 1798; 884 (b), 1580; 885 (c); 886 (b); 887 (d); 888 (d), (a), (b), (c); 889 (c); 890 1b, 2d, 3a, 4c; 891 (d); 892 (b); 893 (c), in Preface to *Mademoiselle de Maupin*; 894 (c); 895 (a); 896 (a); 897 (c); 898 1c, 2d, 3b, 4a; 899 (c); 900 (b); 901 (a); 902 (b); 903 (b), 8: 21-22, (c) 9: 60; 904 (b), 15: 15-17; 905 (b), 8: 36; 906 (a), (b), (c); 907 (b); 908 (a); 909 (a), (d); 910 (c); 911 (b); 912 (a), 6:7; 913 (c); 914 (d),18:37-38; 915 (c), 1:2; 916 (c), 2:10; 917 (b), 19:24; 918 (d), 15:11-32; 919 (a), 26:15, 27: 3-5; 920 (c), 9:1; 921all; 922 (d), I Kings 11:1-8; 923 (d), 14:2; 924 (c); 12:12; 925 (a), 5:39; 926 (a), 3:19; 927 (b); 928 (d), 10:1; 929 (c), 13:24; 930 (a), 7:13-14, (c) 13:24; 931 (a), (c), (d); 932 (a); 933 (b); 934 (b); 935 (d), Genesis 5:21-27; 936 (c), 23:23; 937 (a), 137: 1, The Prayer Book has 'the waters'; 938 (b); 939 (a); 940 (d); 941 (c); 942 (b), 5th century B.C. ; 943 (c); 944 (b); 945 (d), 1:16; 946 (c) 4: 23; 947 (c); 948 (d); 949 (b), 10:30-37; 950 (c); 951 (a); 952 (c); 953 (c); 954 (b); 955 (d); 956 (a); 957 (b); 958 (a); 959 (c); 960 (d); 961 (d); 962 (d); 963 (b); 964 (b); 965 (c); 966 (d); 967 (d); 968 (a); 969 (c); 970 (c); 971 (d); 972 (c); 973 (c); 974 (a); 975 (c), formulated Grimm's Law; 976 (a); 977 1b, 2c, 3a, 4d; 978 (b); 979 (a); 980 (a); 981 (c); 982 (a); 983 (d); 984 (d); 985 (d); 986 (b); 987 (a); 988 (b); 989 (d); 990 (d); 991 (c); 992 (d); 993 (c); 994 (c); 995 (c); 996 (a); 997 (b); 998 (b); 999 (d); 1000 (c).

1a: 1 & (d), 2&(a), 3 & (b) 4 & (c). Of course, 1 &3 and (b) & (d) are interchangeable; 2a (d); 3a (c); 4a all; 5a (a); 6a (d); 7a (a); 8a (b); 9a (d); 10a (c); 11a (c); 12a (c); 13a (c); 14a (c), (d), (a), (b); 15a (c); 16a (c); 17a (c), (d), (b), (a); 18a (c), in 'Home Thoughts from Abroad'; 19a (d); 20a (a), in 'The Betrothed'; 21a (d); 22a (d); 23a (c); 24a (a).

The painting on the cover is by William Hogarth. *A Rake's Progress: The Tavern Scene*, c. 1735.